Just Solitary Me

~

REGINA FELTY

<h1 style="text-align:center">Prologue</h1>

"GROWING OLD IS MANDATORY. GROWING UP IS OPTIONAL."

I read somewhere that Walt Disney said those words, but no one knows for sure. But even if they aren't Walt's words, I bet he agreed with the philosophy. Coming from a man who lived in a world of animated cartoons and amusement parks with larger-than-life Disney characters strolling about the grounds, it's easy to see why he might think growing up is optional.

I'd think that, too, if my world revolved around Disneyland: The Happiest Place on Earth.

My parents took me to Disneyland when I was five years old, and there was nothing magical about it for me. When Snow White came striding over to me in Fantasyland, my parents told me that I went berserk and tried to bite her. Mom was horrified by the crowd that gathered as I screamed and kicked like a feral animal until my dad had to drag me behind a snow cone cart to calm me down. My parents steered me far away from any more costumed employees for the rest of the day. I haven't been back since.

Growing up.

As a kid, I thought it meant I'd fall asleep one night and wake up the next morning as an adult-sized princess adorned in a beautiful gown with layers and layers of satin. Or I'd be something more practical, like a teacher or mail carrier, when I awoke in the grown-up world.

But it hasn't been that easy at all. Growing up has felt like a kitten clawing its way up a tree or a seedling pushing through dry clay, emerging battered and twisted from its harrowing journey.

And I'm not even done growing up yet. Surely it gets easier from here, right?

Chapter One

West Morrison High is proud to announce this year's valedictorian: Brynne Patterson. Brynne has devoted long hours and dedication to her studies to receive this high recognition. The valedictorian of the graduating class is the student with the highest weighted grade point average.

I NIBBLE ON THE END OF MY BEEF JERKY AND READ OVER THE entry again, not sure if I'm wording it just right, because, well, it's not every day that I get to write about a high school graduation—at least not one that I'm actually going to be participating in.

Mr. Porter, my journalism teacher, assigned me to write an article for the school newspaper, the *Morrison Tribute,* about this year's valedictorian and salutatorian. I'm extra stoked about the assignment because my amazing friend, Brynne, is the valedictorian.

Brynne and I are pretty much inseparable these days, always hanging out either at my house or hers. We also go to church together. But we haven't gotten to the place where I can call Brynne my best friend. We've been really close for months now, but I'll always think of Tessa as holding the coveted title of "best friend" even though I haven't seen her in weeks.

My stomach tightens as I push away from my desk and make my way over to the lone window in my room. Three days of rainstorms with their constant *tap, tap, tap* against the roof is enough to drive me crazy in this house. Rain usually makes me feel calm and inspired, which was why I thought this evening would be the perfect time to get some writing done. But, today, the rainfall makes me feel depressed and hopeless, like I want to ram my head into the wall to make it stop.

I press my forehead against the cold glass and try to see through the rivers flowing down its surface. The relentless streaks pouring down the glass and pooling in the cracks of the outer wood frame accurately express what's locked up tight inside of me. I wish I could flip a switch and make the dam release, but I can't.

I just can't.

"Is Tessa gonna be okay, God?" I whisper, and my breath forms a small circle of fog on the glass. Breathing in the heavy damp air of the storm, I draw a finger down the center of the glass and wipe the moisture from my skin onto my sleeve.

I hear a soft knock on my door before it opens and my mom pushes her head through, the scents of fresh garlic and basil drifting in with her. I turn and scowl, not appreciating the intrusion on my private moment.

"Mom, I could've been naked!"

"Sorry," she whispers, although I don't know why she feels the need to whisper. "I thought you were sleeping because you were so quiet in here. I can usually hear the floor creak when you're moving around." She pushes a shoulder through and leans against the door frame. "I just came to tell you dinner will be ready in twenty minutes."

My initial reaction was harsh, I know. I smile so she knows I'm not mad. "It's okay. You just caught me by surprise."

Brows creased into a deep frown, she gives me that look that moms give when they can tell something is wrong. There's no getting out of it either; she's gonna ask.

"Are you okay?"

That's a loaded question, and she knows it. I haven't been okay since Tessa went missing that night and we didn't know what happened for months, only to have Tessa come home—*Thank God*—alive, but as fragile as a cracked vase. The same girl I've known and been best friends with since second grade is no longer the Tessa I once knew. I hardly recognize the girl who loved to visit thrift stores and was always talking me into one shenanigan after another.

No, nothing has felt "okay" since I watched Tessa leave that party—*Drunk? High?*—and get in the car with three strange guys. And I didn't try to stop her. Oh, I made a weak attempt to get her attention before she brushed me off that night, but I still feel like I could've done more.

I've had all the conversations with my parents, her parents, the police, the school counselor, my youth pastor—you name it—and they all assure me that it wasn't my fault and that Tessa made her own choices. But none of it makes the guilt and heartbreak go away or makes me feel "okay" again.

"I'm fine, Mom."

Yeah, I told a big, fat lie. *Sorry, God . . . I'm trying.*

She opens her mouth like she's about to call me out, but doesn't.

"I love you, Alli."

Before I can respond—or burst out in tears, which is more likely—Mom slips back out the door as quietly as she came in. She knew that's all I really needed to hear.

I glance back at the glowing screen of my laptop where my article sits waiting for me to finish it, but I've lost interest.

The smell of garlic and basil that's been lingering in the air now mingles with the rich aroma of homemade tomato sauce and is calling to me. There's no resisting Dad's homemade manicotti, so I don't even bother trying.

I slam my laptop closed as I pass and whisper, "Let's try this again later, alright?"

Chapter Two

"Hey, Alli!"

I spin around to see Brynne making her way toward me, a huge, overstuffed green binder pressed to her chest. Several brown curls hang free from her high ponytail and bounce around her face as she hurries down the hall. I was reaching for the door to the counselor's office when she called me.

She stops in front of me, and I feel the energy radiating off of her. Her pastel pink blazer complements her flushed cheeks perfectly as she takes a moment to catch her breath. She glances around before pinning me with a curious stare. Her eyebrows lift as she jerks her head toward the door where the guidance counselor's name—Mrs. Arroyo—is printed in bold letters on a wood plaque hanging on the wall.

"Are you in trouble or something?"

I lean in, giving her my best concerned look. "Well, to be honest, I didn't want to tell you, but Mrs. Arroyo called me in to talk about your grades. They miscalculated your GPA, and you actually fell short of making valedictorian." I bite my lip for emphasis, looking appropriately sympathetic. "She didn't want to tell you herself and thought it might be better if I broke it to you . . ."

The *bonk* on my head with her binder comes out of nowhere. "Oh, knock it off, Alli." She laughs. "What are you *really* doing here?"

I rub the sting at my hairline. "Well, if you *must* know, Ms. Nosey, she's giving me scholarship paperwork to fill out for college in the fall. Some of us have to work a lot harder to get into college, you know." I scowl at the binder in her hands.

"You just need to get your head out of the clouds, Alli Mancini, and be more like Yours Truly." Brynne tosses her head and brushes my shoulder as she moves on down the hall. Then, she turns back and bats her eyes at me.

I stick my tongue out. "You're such a snob, Brynne."

I open the office door just as I hear her say, "And you admire me anyway."

Rolling my eyes, I step forward and pull the door closed behind me.

Mrs. Arroyo's office smells like a medley of sweet orange, vanilla, and something akin to cinnamon, which gives me the sensation of walking into a gourmet chocolate shop. I spy the wood diffuser with its clear glass dome sitting in the corner. A lazy loop of mist snakes out of its mouth and migrates my way. Several teachers have diffusers and wax burners in their rooms since lit candles are banned on campus for obvious reasons. Some days, the intoxicating mixture of scents from class to class can be nauseating.

But today, I inhale the scent of the room and instantly crave a cranberry orange truffle from See's Candy. Every Christmas, I ask my parents for my very own box of truffles from See's Candy, and I don't share a single bite. I glance down at my watch to see if it's anywhere close to lunch time.

10:45. Nope.

"Come on in, mija!"

Mrs. Arroyo enters from a small side room and flashes a radiant smile. The long string of brightly colored beads that makes up her daily attire sways from side to side across her ample, round belly as she hurries over. The beads remind me of old photos of my mom in her hippie days. Mrs. Arroyo shuffles closer, and her shoes drag assertively over the worn carpet. Her golden cheeks are tinged scarlet from the effort, but that doesn't affect her bubbly persona one bit.

"How are you today, honey?" She says it like we haven't talked in years instead of just two days ago. I finish signing my name on the clipboard and tap the pen back down into its holder.

"I'm doing good, Mrs. Arroyo. I just came to pick up the scholarship papers you have for me."

She crooks a finger at me and lumbers over to her desk, her long black hair swaying across her back with the same rhythm as her beads. As I trail behind her, I can't help but glance down at her feet, jammed into black patent leather heels with no nylons and wonder if she ever gets blisters. Pulling out the heavy wood chair in front of her desk, I lower myself into it. It wobbles so badly that I have to grip the edge of her desk to keep from toppling over. I let my backpack slide off my shoulder to the floor.

It takes several grunts before Mrs. Arroyo coaxes the rolling chair closer to her desk. Then, she starts moving folders around, shifting piles from one side of her desk to the other, looking for my paperwork, I assume.

Most of the kids I know at West Morrison High School say they don't like coming to see Mrs. Arroyo about anything personal because she always claims teenagers are dramatic and exaggerate everything. Staring at her monstrously long false eyelashes and her Mardi Gras–worthy beads, I wonder who's actually more dramatic.

"Ah, got it!" She says triumphantly.

From under a mountain of manila folders and a file box, Mrs. Arroyo tugs out a large, white envelope, checks the information on the front, and slides it across the desk toward me. "Here you go. Take it home and look it over with your parents. If you need my help with the application or have any questions, just let me know."

She fingers her beads as she smiles at me. "Are you ready for California?"

She's referring to the University of Southern California, where I plan to pursue a degree in journalism. My parents aren't thrilled with the idea of me moving to California; they think it's way too liberal and are sure I'm gonna be brainwashed into becoming a communist or something. That and they wanted me to live close enough for us to drive back and forth for weekend visits. But they know USC has a great journalism program, which is high on my priority list.

However, what I haven't told my parents yet is that I'm still trying to figure out if I even *want* to go to college. And I don't plan on mentioning that to them or Mrs. Arroyo yet.

"Yeah, it's a lot to think about right now, but"—I tap my finger on the envelope in front of me—"I can't put it off any longer. Thanks so much for your help with this, Mrs. Arroyo."

I lift the envelope in one hand while pushing myself out of the hazardous chair with the other and imagine her batting lashes following me out of the room as I rush out in a cloud of orange and vanilla.

Chapter Three

"How's the paperwork coming along?"

Mom looks over her shoulder at me from the counter, where she's pouring a cup of coffee. My answer comes out somewhere between a growl and a grumble.

"Oh, sounds like it's going well." She laughs. "Need some help?"

I push the stack of college applications to the side and pull my laptop closer. "I can do a lot of it online, but I'm trying to fill in some of the answers on paper first. I haven't even started on the essay portion yet."

Mom carries over a plate of homemade cinnamon rolls and sets them down in front of me. "What's the essay topic about?"

"Me," I say.

"You?"

I stuff the corner of a roll in my mouth, chew briefly, then lick icing off my fingers. "Yeah, obviously they want to know what I plan to do with my future, but the main focus is writing an essay about myself. They want some personal insight into who I am and what my interests are. The minimum word count is six hundred words."

"Well, how hard can that be? You spit out more words than that with half of the articles you write for the school newspaper. Besides, who doesn't like to talk about themselves?"

I know Mom's trying to be encouraging, but I'm not catching her enthusiasm.

"Uh, yeah, I know but . . . it's about *me.* Have you ever tried to write six hundred words about yourself, Mom?"

Cinnamon roll poised in air, Mom gives me a reflective look. "Well, isn't it sort of like a résumé?"

"Really? A résumé? No, Mom. This isn't just making a bullet list of my work history—which I have none of anyway—or special qualifications. They want me to write about what I want to do with my future and what inspires me in life. How can I write about stuff I'm not even sure about myself?"

"Start with what inspires you. That should be easy," she says. "You love to write, so what kinds of things inspire your writing?"

I look down at my laptop, as if the inspiration will jump off the screen at me. "Well, I like digging into people's experiences and writing about real events. More along the lines of investigative journalism, you know? But it's not like there's a whole lot of scandals or corruption in high school to write about, although I do think there is some credence to the conspiracy theory that the cafeteria ladies are hoarding all the good food for themselves and dishing out leftovers for lunch."

Mom chuckles at that one. "But," I continue, "once in a while, I get in a creative mood and attempt to write a fiction piece."

"Okay, so that's a start—not the part about writing fiction. You can't make up stories about yourself." She wags one finger in the air. "So go with real life experiences, researching, uncovering the truth about things . . . Expand on that a bit. Of course, I wouldn't recommend mentioning anything about cafeteria ladies. You might scare them off with that." Mom smiles. "And just because I'm curious about your fiction writing—what inspires you with that?"

"Again, I have to be in a creative mood to write it," I say with a shrug. "If I waited for inspiration though, I'd never get anything worthwhile written. I better stick with what I know I'm good at."

A thoughtful expression crosses Mom's face. "And what about the other part of your essay?"

"What other part?" I ask.

"The part where you write about what you want to do with your future."

"Well, like I said, I'm still not sure about that yet. But I have an idea."

"And . . . ?" The look she gives me tells me that she's curious about more than just how I'm gonna pull this whole essay off. She's prying to learn more about what my plans might be for my future.

I lock eyes with her and lower the rest of my cinnamon roll back to the plate. "To be honest, Mom, I don't think you're gonna like my answer."

"Try me," she says, but I note the hesitancy in her eyes. Like she wants to know but also might *not* want to know.

I take my time answering, drawing in several deep breaths before I let the words come.

"I know I want to do something different. Something I've never tried before that's far away from Tucson. Not that I don't love you guys and all," I hurry to assure her. "It's just that, you know, after everything that's happened this year . . ."

Mom thinks I'm only referring to the slowly dissolving friendship between Tessa and me and the obvious traumatic experience of Tessa's kidnapping and recovery. But it's more than that.

I'm grateful, for Tessa's sake, that she's been in therapy and working through the horrors of her ordeal, and I know she has a long way to go still in the healing process, but I've never felt like I've been able to move on or that I've really healed from it all myself.

I don't tell my mom that though. I just let her believe

that I'm just feeling burdened about friendship problems and worrying about Tessa.

I'm the only one who knows that the pain goes deeper for me, like a tiny flame that's steadily being fanned into a ball of fire with every breath. I haven't told *anyone* how I struggle with what happened to Tessa because it would draw attention to me when she's the one who needs it most. And, honestly, it's easier to deal with the struggle alone rather than draw everyone's focus to my guilt and make me feel worse than I already do.

My parents and I met with my pastor several times after Tessa returned home, and he mentioned something about survivor's guilt. I didn't pay much attention to the term at the time because it sounded like some professional jargon adults just threw out there to make them sound more knowledgeable. I know our pastor and my parents meant well and were just trying to help, but I never felt our conversations made me feel any better—or any less guilty.

I don't know, maybe that's my fault.

To be fair, they did most of the talking, and I refused to do any. At the time, I didn't see the point. I felt like the only one I needed to talk to about what was bothering me and who had all the answers was God. I decided long ago that was a safer route for me.

As I look back now, it never dawned on me that God doesn't make a habit out of writing on walls and speaking from clouds, but that he uses people in our lives to be his voice of reason and healing. Maybe I've drawn out everything I've been struggling with and questioning more than I needed to when I might have felt much better had I shared it with someone else. That's exactly what I've been trying to get through to Tessa for a while now: It's time to talk about it. Maybe it's time for me to listen to my own advice.

Mom's voice pulls my drifting thoughts back. "And you think that moving away will make it better?"

"What do you mean?"

She sets her roll down on a small plate that had somehow appeared in front of her and wipes the tips of her fingers delicately on the edge of a napkin.

"Exactly what I said. You believe that running away from hard things here will make things easier for you when you get there—wherever *there* ends up taking you."

I can't understand why she isn't getting this. Even if she doesn't know the depth of my feelings, she's more than aware of everything else I've been going through these past months.

"Isn't it obvious, Mom? Getting out of Tucson is the best choice for me. I won't be around snobs and people who can't help but point out how eccentric they think I am just because of my faith. I can make new friends in a different youth group, and I won't have guilt hanging over my head like I feel every time I have to look at . . ." I can't say it, knowing that I've said more than I wanted to already.

I had expected Mom to have a shocked looked on her face, or at least roll her eyes at me for acting so dramatic.

But what I notice instead is a look of pity that makes my insides squirm.

"First off, I know there are lots of people who are Christians who don't live exactly like we do, but *eccentric* doesn't describe you at all." She smiles softly.

By *live like we do*, she's referring to the fact that, as Apostolic Christian women, we wear skirts and dresses and don't wear makeup and jewelry.

"So let me get this straight," she says, turning serious. "If you can pull up roots here, you'll be able to replant yourself someplace where there are no rude people, no one that judges you for being a Christian, and no broken people? All of your friends—your *new* friends—will have no flaws, and you'll be walking on cloud nine from there on out. Does that sound about right?" Mom lifts her cinnamon roll to her lips with two fingers. "If so, I need to find a place like that for myself."

I feel my face warm. "That's not what I mean, Mom."

"Oh, what do you mean, then?" She says, her tongue sliding across her lips, collecting loose crumbs.

I push my laptop and plate away, the remainder of my snack forgotten.

"I feel like I've been boxed in here, Mom. Everyone knows me as a nice Christian girl who doesn't say a word to defend herself. Not only that, but they'll also never let me live down—"

I almost say "the Chad ordeal" but catch myself. My mom doesn't know about my sneaking out to run around with Chad Barton and how he ended up shattering my heart and what little reputation I still had intact.

"—going to that party and how things ended up for Tessa. It's not that I feel they blame me for what happened but . . . it's just the fact that I'm not the kind of girl that goes to parties as it is, and then I was one of the last people to see Tessa that night . . ." My voice trails off to a whisper, heat flooding my cheeks.

How can I expect Mom to understand the full depth of my anguish when she only knows half the story?

Part of me wishes she knew about the roller-coaster ride of emotions with Chad that ended in a crash and how much Shanice and Kim have gone out of their way to make my life miserable every chance they get. I wish I could unload the awful burden I carry knowing about Tessa's abortion and the guilt of wondering if I should have spent more energy trying to reach out to her instead of seeking retribution, trying to prove my worth to some guy, and behaving like someone I wasn't. I brought a lot of hurt on myself by my choices. So much so that I couldn't find it in me to be strong for someone else.

I feel Mom's hand rest on mine, her thumb rubbing the back of my hand in a soothing gesture. "I'm sorry, Alli. I had no idea how much you've had on your shoulders all these months. I wish you'd have felt you could have confided in me."

I don't know why but, instead of comforting me, all I feel is a wave of condemnation over making my mom feel bad. That hadn't been my intention at all. I imagine how much worse she would have felt if she knew the full extent of everything that I've struggled with all this time. If she knew, she'd be on the phone with our pastor first thing in the morning, setting up another counseling session. To say I'd be mortified would be an understatement.

Mustering up my bravest smile, I give Mom's hand a squeeze. "It's okay, Mom. I'm doing fine. Honest. It's just that I think a change of scenery would do me good. Besides, we've always known that I might go off to college someday."

The look she gives me makes my chest feel like there's a bowling ball lodged behind my rib cage. I have a hard time getting a full breath. Moms have this extra instinct that reveals exactly the thing you're trying so hard to hide from them. I squirm as I feel the weight of her stare, inspecting and analyzing my words as if she's an archaeologist brushing away layers of dust from a newly discovered relic.

"Yes, you're right, honey. We've talked several times about the possibility that you'd go away to college. But I don't think a degree in journalism is the real reason you want to go." Her words drive home the point that she'd solved the mystery behind my feeble attempt to bury my secrets. "I believe the real reason you want to leave is because you are running from your problems and things you don't want to face anymore, and that's the worst decision you can make in this case. You know what I'm going to ask, right?"

Yes, I know exactly what she's gonna ask because it's what most of our serious conversations eventually lead up to. I'll tell her what she wants to hear and, although I won't be lying, I won't be completely honest either because I've only given it a half-hearted attempt.

"Yes, Mom, I've prayed about it and will keep praying. I just haven't felt any answers come back yet."

Chapter Four

I'M IN A DAZE AS I WATCH ZACH PULL OUT THREE DIFFERENT colored highlighters for our science lecture. He never ceases to amaze me, as well as irritate me, with his overachieving efficiency.

"I hate you, Zach."

When he stops mid-highlighter-placement and stares at me in shock, my face must show I'm teasing because he shakes his head and lays the green marker down between the yellow and blue ones. "You might try taking notes once in a while, Alli."

Wow. Must have hit a nerve.

"Touché, Zach," whispers a voice nearby.

Brynne smirks at me from across the table and jabs a finger down at her notebook. That's when I notice that, next to her science notebook, she has highlighters laid out as well, though not as meticulously organized as Zach's.

"Whatever," I mouth to her. I get the hint and start hunting for markers in my backpack, hoping I have at least one that isn't dried out.

I'm buried inside my backpack when I hear something roll across the table. Peering over the top of my bag, I watch a yellow marker roll to a stop in front of me. I glance at Brynne, but she's looking toward the front of the room, where Mr. Martin has started writing on the whiteboard.

"You better hurry up."

My eyes dart to Zach, who points at the marker, shrugs, and turns his attention to Mr. Martin. Pushing the backpack to the floor, I jerk open my notebook and grab my pencil. I don't know whether to be grateful or intimidated to be sitting at the same table with two Einsteins.

Somehow, I manage to keep up with Mr. Martin—who's notorious for lecturing at warp-speed—and am just highlighting the last vocabulary word in my notes when he announces that there are homework worksheets on the back table for us to collect on our way out. Capping the marker, I hold it out to Zach.

"Thanks, Zach. You saved me."

"Keep it," he says. He probably just doesn't feel like unzipping his backpack to put it away, or maybe he thinks it's contaminated with my slacker vibes and might infect him with bad grades. It's probably for the best since I'm sure I don't have a decent marker to use for the rest of the week anyway.

The bell rings and Zach and I make our way to grab

our homework sheets. Before reaching the back of the room, I notice Shanice standing in front of Brynne at the worksheet table.

If there was ever a person put on this earth to be my sandpaper, it's Shanice Bradshaw: co-captain of the cheer team, classic smart mouth, and one of the few people who I've come close to legitimately hating. Not only did she contaminate and lure Tessa away from me when Tessa joined the cheer team and took up with Shanice's crowd, but she makes it her objective to ridicule my faith every chance she gets.

I avoid her like the plague.

The way Shanice looks at Brynne right now as she talks makes it appear that she's scolding a toddler. Brynne's back is to me, so I have no idea what's happening on her side. I'm in no hurry to walk up on them, knowing that I'll probably be dragged into something I don't want to be part of, but I can't avoid approaching since Brynne is blocking the stack of homework sheets that Zach and I need access to.

When Brynne turns my way, I don't have time to look down and act like I wasn't watching, so it doesn't take much for Brynne to catch my eye. Expecting to see anger or frustration, I'm ready to launch into an interrogation, asking, "What did she say to you?" But Brynne is smiling. *Smiling*. I can't remember either one of us ever having a run-in with Shanice and walking away with a smile on our face—not once.

Just as I reach her, Brynne hands me a paper. "Got one for you."

I'm slow about taking it because I'm still processing the *why* regarding the smile on Brynne's face.

"What was *that* all about?" I ask, nodding toward Shanice's retreating back.

Brynne glances at Shanice, then back to me. "Oh, just typical Shanice. She asked if I'm a 'holy roller' now. I told her I have no clue what she's talking about and that *she* probably doesn't know what she's talking about either. What on earth is a *holy roller*?" She mutters. "Anyhow, I invited her to church on Sunday." Brynne grins and wiggles her eyebrows, like we share a secret body language code that I'm supposed to know about. I'm still not seeing what she's so cheerful about. In fact, I'm ready to choke on my spit.

"You seriously invited her to *church*?" I screech. "And, for your information, her use of *holy roller* wasn't a compliment."

Most of the others have already exited the room, but the few who are left stare over at us. I ignore them. My stomach lurches, remembering earlier this year when a girl from church—Kristin—and I were handing out flyers for an upcoming youth rally and ran into Shanice and two other cheerleaders. One of them was Kim, the cheer captain and basically Shanice's puppet master.

Kristin and I were a big, fat joke to them, and they messed with us the whole time. Kristin was oblivious to what they were doing and kept jabbering on and on about the rally until I literally dragged her away, giving them more fuel for the fire. I was completely mortified and furious with Kristin for making us look stupid.

Could Brynne really be that gullible? I wonder.

Brynne should know better. She's already had a taste of Shanice's scorn, like the time Shanice showed up at the bookstore when some of us were having a Bible study and ridiculed us. Brynne had engaged Shanice then as well, treating her as if she wasn't the snake that we all know Shanice is. I'm not as angry with Brynne for engaging Shanice as much as I was with Kristin, but I can't help being more than a little miffed about why they keep doing it.

"Sure, why not invite her?" Brynne says. "Everyone deserves to hear about God, Alli, even one of West Morrison High School's elite."

"Yeah, right. *Elite.*"

I'm aware that my attitude is showing on my face and in my voice, and I make an attempt to soften both. "Fine," I sigh. "You're right, I know, but . . . *Shanice?* Why her? We all know she doesn't have the least interest in going to church, Brynne. She's just collecting steam for her next drama show."

Brynne looks confused for a moment—probably trying to figure out what my problem is—before she takes a deep breath and continues, sounding like she's patiently trying to explain something to a young child, which, I know, is exactly how I'm acting right now.

"Alli, I get that you don't like Shanice and that she's treated you—treated *us*—like trash," she says, leading the way as we walk out of class. "But you gotta be bigger than that. It's our, I don't know, *job* to show her the love of Jesus and not let her get under our skin."

Brynne jumps ahead of me and stops, blocking my way and forcing me to stop and give her my full attention. "You know this already, Alli. Weren't you the one that taught me that in the first place?" Giving me a quick hug, she veers off to her next class.

I just stare after her.

Why are new Christians so overenthusiastic?

The stab of guilt comes immediately because I know Brynne is absolutely right. Her attitude—new Christian enthusiasm and all—is spot on, and my attitude is totally wrong.

But I can't help it. I just *know* Shanice just wants to stir up drama, and, now, Brynne just gave her something to start with.

Chapter Five

IT's BIBLE STUDY NIGHT AT THE BOOKSTORE WITH BRYNNE and Anthony, who leads our group and study sessions, and I don't want to go.

Since Brynne's innocent-but-bound-to-backfire invitation to Shanice to come to church, I've noticed that every time Shanice and her friends are around, they're looking our way and appear to be either amused or sneering. There's no telling what Shanice is cooking up, and I wouldn't put it past her to make another appearance at the bookstore tonight just to make trouble.

And I'm not up to the possibility of that challenge tonight.

So far, Anthony hasn't been around when Shanice decides to show up, but I'm fairly sure his reaction would be the same as Brynne's. In fact, he'd probably pull out his Bible and start witnessing to her on the spot. Naturally, I'd be horror-stricken and probably crawl under the table if that happened. I guess I'll never be the poster child for the "Best Christian Ever" campaign, if there ever was one.

Somehow, I seem to always end up being part of the target that Shanice zeroes in on, and I'm over it. If I can keep myself out of sight as much as possible, that's what I plan to do. And that's why I don't want to go tonight.

Lame. I get it.

Brynne and Anthony don't know Shanice and her kind as well as I do. They weren't the target when she and her friends talked Chad—West Morrison's football icon and known heartthrob—into pranking me by acting like he was all into me before I discovered a text on his phone that revealed he was just using me as part of a dare and to provide entertainment for all his friends. I can't imagine how it would have all ended up for me if I hadn't seen that text. It was an ugly enough ending as it was and took me months to get over. I'm still not entirely over it.

Snatching my phone off the dresser, I throw myself down against a pile of bed pillows. It doesn't take me long to tap out an excuse and hit *send* in a group text to Brynne and Anthony.

I don't wait around for their replies, which I know are coming. I drop the phone on the bed and make my way to the kitchen to dig up a snack. Thankfully, my mom and Avery went to a see a play with Mom's best friend tonight or I'd have to explain why I'm not going to Bible study to Mom too.

I'm pretty sure all females memorize scripts when they become mothers, and mine is no exception. I know to expect the standard, "How was your night?" or "What did you learn?" from Mom tonight, but I plan to be in bed before she and Avery arrive home. More than likely, she'll forget the script before I see her again tomorrow night: *Bravo to me!*

I shuffle around inside the pantry until I spy the opened box of Cheez-Its behind some cans of beans.

"Score!" I say to an audience of canned goods and canisters of rice and pasta. I scoop up a jar of creamy peanut butter and push the pantry door closed with my hip. Grabbing a plate from a cabinet, I load it high with Cheez-Its and a big scoop of peanut butter—my favorite snack combo—and grab a cherry-flavored water from the refrigerator.

Just as I'm pouring the water into a glass of ice, I hear it. The familiar *ding* from my phone in the bedroom. I grab my plate and glass and head to the back porch, where I won't be able to hear any more notifications from my phone. It's the best I can do to escape the reality of my lameness. I know I can't ignore it forever, but I can at least enjoy my food in peace for a few minutes.

The back porch is quiet and relaxing as I dip my Cheez-Its in the gooey peanut butter and watch our neighbor build a wooden storage shed in his backyard. But I'm feeling far from relaxed as I worry about what I'm gonna tell Brynne tomorrow at school when she asks if I got my article for journalism done, since that's what I told her and Anthony I had to stay home and work on tonight.

I do have that article on the school library upgrades to work on and a little more to finish up on the graduation piece, but both aren't due for another week. Gathering my empty plate and glass, I plod back into the house, determined to write a few lines for the library article so I'm not completely lying.

After washing my dish and refilling my drink, basically stalling having to read the text that I know is probably from Brynne, I finally make my way to my room. I glance at the phone on my bed, then decide to run to the bathroom before settling down to drop a few lines on my article to make things official. Before I leave for the bathroom, though, there is another *ding* from my phone.

Fine. Whatever.

I grab the phone from the bed and plop down into my desk chair. Not bothering to read the lock-screen notification, I swipe to unlock the screen and tap on the message icon. Predictably, the message is from Brynne.

> Oh, bummer. It was my turn to treat coffee
> tonight too. :(You can't just come for thirty
> minutes?

There's another text after Brynne's. This one from Anthony.

> No prob. We understand. See you Friday night!

It strikes me that it might be awkward for the two of them tonight with me not there. To someone walking by, it might look like they are on a date or something. Anthony is super touchy about how things might seem to other people, even if he and Brynne are meeting in a public place and all. That's just Anthony for you.

Oh well, they'll figure it out.

I text out a quick message:

> Sorry, Brynne. Can't tonight. See u both on Friday though!

Putting aside the phone—and my conscience—I open my laptop and tap on the file labeled *library_art* and get to work. Five minutes of this, then I can read a couple chapters of my new mystery novel.

The night is looking more promising already.

Chapter Six

I stare down at the faded gray hoodie in my hand.

For a moment, I'm frozen in a snapshot of a past time: Tessa and I draped across her bed, giggling over some YouTube video that she found. All I can remember about it was that there were two girls trying to push each other into a lake, laughing so hard that they both ended up falling in. I remember Tessa looking up from the video and over at me. She plucked on my sleeve and said, "Hey! That's my hoodie!"

"Yeah, you loaned it to me, dork," I told her.

"That was, like, three weeks ago!"

I promised to bring it back after I washed it. Obviously, that never happened since I just discovered the long-forgotten hoodie in the back of my closet. I sigh and set it down on the bed. I'll surprise Tessa with it when I go over for dinner tonight.

It's been three months since Tessa escaped from her captors, and I can't help but feel a fresh stab in my heart every time I see her. I was there that night—the night we were at a party, and I saw her with two guys who I knew didn't go to our school and who I'd never seen around Tessa before. It was obvious that she wasn't herself and that something was off about her behavior. I honestly tried to distract her and get her away from those guys, but they hovered over her like two wolves guarding their prey.

I suspected—and now know for sure—that they'd slipped something into her drink. It was the only possible way they would've been able to coax Tessa into leaving the party and getting into the car with them. By the time I decided that I needed to get some help, it was too late. They'd driven off with Tessa, and that was the last time I'd seen her.

Tessa wasn't heard from for two months, the most agonizing two months any of us had ever endured. Her family, her friends, other people at the party—none of us had any idea where she was or what had happened. And since I was the last person to see her leave that party with those guys, I felt the weight of guilt every waking moment.

I've replayed the reel of that night over and over again in my mind, and although I assure myself that I tried to get her away from those two creeps and Tessa blew me off, I still feel like I should have been more aggressive with my effort. Then again, what more *could* I have done, short of tackling Tessa? Would that have gotten her attention, or would those guys have possibly hurt me instead?

Everyone in the community joined in the search for Tessa. Every lead and anonymous tip was followed, but no one really knew where she'd been taken or if she'd gone willingly. The investigators questioned her friends and family while tactfully suggesting that Tessa may have planned her disappearance and was simply a runaway. Since Tessa's parents had recently gone through a divorce and things at home were strained, the runaway suspicion took root the longer she was gone.

It was only my testimony that cast doubt on her running away. I was adamant that she wasn't acting herself at the party, that I'd seen Tessa drunk before and how I saw her behave that night wasn't the same.

"Besides, who runs away and doesn't take any personal possessions with them?" I told them, including the fact that she left her purse and phone behind at the party. Most seemed to agree, but others shook their heads in doubt.

Then, my dad got the phone call from Paul, Tessa's dad. Tessa had escaped. The local police in New Mexico received a frantic call from Tessa, who had called from a payphone, and had picked her up.

She told the police that she'd gotten away from her captors when she and two other girls who shared a room with her broke the lock and fled in the middle of the night. The three of them stayed together until they got closer to a crowded area, some little town that I can't remember the name of, and then split up in case someone saw them. According to Tessa, she didn't know where the two other girls were now or if they'd even made it to safety. The police were still searching for the girls' whereabouts.

Dad, Mom, and I were in Dad's office when the call came. We hugged and cried tears of joy together at the news. We gave a prayer of thanks to God that she was alive and that she was coming home. When we met up with Tessa's family later that night, we all cried together. Calls were made to church members, neighbors, and more, and the tears flowed over and over again. Our tears were like a healing balm to our hearts.

But healing wouldn't come that easy for Tessa.

Two months of being held against her will and abused in ways that will forever haunt her nightmares had left Tessa with scars that forever changed the girl we'd all known and loved. I still love Tessa—that will never change. But I can't show her that love without her recoiling.

I understand. It's something I've had to learn to accept.

Tessa never reaches out to me or lets me past the iron-clad walls she's erected, and I don't blame her after all she's been through. Honestly, we weren't talking all that much before it happened, so the walls were already in place.

I guess a part of me thought that none of what happened between us would matter now that she was home safe and that we'd pick up where we left off before cheerleading and parties got in the way of our friendship. But I was mistaken to believe it could be that simple, and I'm learning the hard way that broken people can't be put back together overnight.

Tessa and I had been best friends since second grade. Our friendship grew from giggling in class in elementary school, to junior high boy crazes, to all the drama that comes with high school. But something shifted in our relationship when Tessa made the cheer team earlier this school year and started hanging out with a new group of friends.

I guess that wouldn't have been a big deal under normal circumstances. I mean, we've never been territorial over each other or gotten mad if one of us hung out with other people. But by the way she shut me out and cozied up to her new upper-class crowd, it was obvious that she'd either outgrown or had gotten tired of me.

But it was more complex than that. It wasn't just that Tessa started hanging out with new friends, but she began acting like them in all the wrong ways and letting them influence her to get involved in some shady stuff. Little by little, Tessa pulled away from me, eventually choosing them over me. It tore me up pretty badly, and there were times when I didn't know if I should cry because I missed her or just let myself hate her. I pretty much ended up doing both, crying one moment and nurturing seething anger the next.

What made things worse for me was that, even though I've been a Christian since Tessa and I became friends as kids, and she'd always stood firm about never wanting to so much as step foot in a church (although I'd managed to successfully bribe her to come a time or two), my faith suddenly became a dividing issue between us.

Tessa had never made a big deal of me being a Christian before. Until, that is, her new uppity friends made a big deal of it, namely two girls on the cheer team: Kim and Shanice. Somehow, I became a target for them to mess with and harass, and Tessa did nothing to defend me, even joining in on the bullying a time or two.

That sealed the fate of our friendship.

Tessa had tapped out and left me trying to make sense of what went wrong between us and how I'd been left with the short end of the stick. Left with injured pride and the pain of rejection, I went on a destructive campaign in an attempt to salvage my self-esteem and show the world that I didn't need Tessa in my life to survive. But, instead of building my case and proving my point, I ended up making impulsive decisions that left me more broken and humiliated than I'd started out as, and it wasn't even Tessa's doing this time.

It took a lot for me to find the courage to go and see Tessa after her horrific ordeal in New Mexico. It wasn't the loss of our friendship over the months prior to her kidnapping that made it so hard for me either. I still cared enough about her to overlook all that. What's a few months being adversaries compared to years of being bosom friends? But the indestructible walls Tessa had built around her now made it almost impossible to reach her.

A soft tap on my bedroom door rattles me from my

stupor. My mom's face appears around the edge of the door as she pushes it open.

"What time will you be home tonight?"

Glancing at the clock and realizing that I need to leave soon if I'm gonna get to Tessa's on time for dinner, I grab my sandals and sit on the bed to put them on.

"Um, not too late. Maybe around 9:00?" I say while trying to manage the tiny buckle on one sandal.

"Okay. Be safe. Love you," she says before closing the door behind her.

I'm bummed that I won't be driving over to Tessa's, now that I have my own wheels. Well, they aren't *my* wheels, they're my dad's old ones. It's nothing fancy or even close to cool for a teenager to drive, but it's functional and gives me some freedom. But Tessa only lives a few houses away, so— freedom or not—it would be ridiculous to drive over there instead of walking.

Sandals secured, I grab my purse from the bed and reach for the light switch. Before I flick the light off, I notice Tessa's hoodie still laying on the bed, snatch it up, and shove it in my purse. At least the forgotten hoodie will give us something to talk about.

Chapter Seven

As I walk the short distance to Tessa's, I try to remember the last time I'd dropped in to see her.

Has it been two weeks since I've even called?

That realization makes me feel awful. I know Tessa doesn't expect me to call or check in on her all the time, but I've made it a goal to do it anyway. It's just that I've been so busy the past few weeks with scholarship paperwork and college applications, that checking in with Tessa has been on the back burner.

It's not just being busy that has made me negligent though.

I hate to admit to myself that it's hard to be around Tessa more and more lately. She's grown so quiet and withdrawn that I'm beginning to feel like I'm intruding and making things worse instead of better. Whenever I'm around her, I leave with a dark cloud hanging over me that takes days to lift. I'm not sure if it's my own inability to cope with what happened to Tessa that's triggered or the fact that I really want to help lift her burden but don't have a clue where to start.

When I went to see Tessa right after she came home, she told me that there's no way I could understand what she went through and that she'd be offended if I dared to say that I knew how she felt.

She was right. It would have been wrong for me to claim that I knew how she felt. I've never had something so awful happen to me or felt the fear and horror that she must've experienced, being forced to participate in things that most of us only encounter in our worst nightmares, her innocence in both mind and body forever stripped from her.

But Tessa's pain and the emotional scars she bore went far deeper than just her horrific experience with being trafficked. Could the dark emotional storms she was already facing have blinded her to what she was walking into that night? How many people, besides me, knew the other dreadful secrets she harbored?

Earlier this year, Tessa had hooked up with a guy from school and ended up pregnant. For a brief window of time, Tessa and I rediscovered the close bond we'd once had as she confided in me.

Even though she had surrounded herself with new

friends, she obviously didn't feel she could turn to them in her lowest moment. I'm sure those who knew her secret had already shoved the abortion option down her throat as her *only* option. And, as I know from my own painful experience, her bogus friends had probably made sport of her "stupidity" and assassinated her character behind her back.

That's why Tessa called me. She knew I'd be there for her, regardless of how far we'd drifted from each other.

And I did have her back. I listened. I cried with her. I prayed for her. But I also naively believed I could help Tessa through it, hard as it was. I believed my support could propel her to make the right decision about her dilemma. But my presumption proved to be flawed.

I guess Tessa's fear trumped any pep talk or support that I could offer. All Tessa seemed to hear were the voices of doubt and fear drowning out all reason until she succumbed and did away with the pregnancy. I could tell by the look on her face the day she told me about it that her decision weighed heavily on her and would likely haunt her for a long time to come.

And being at that party that night and flirting with disaster hadn't been the best choice either. But what happened to Tessa and what was forced on her was *not* her choice. Even as a teenager, I'm mature enough to know that I'm gonna look back on a lot of things that I did and decisions I've made and ask myself, "What were you thinking, Alli?" I'll cringe and shake my head at my mistakes and, hopefully, have learned my lessons well.

But Tessa won't have that luxury.

Sure, she'll look back on some of her fateful decisions and regret them, but having the power of choice stolen from her will be like a cancer eating away at her heart for years into the future. The scars may eventually heal, but there is also a chance they'll sit just below the surface, vulnerable to being reopened.

Arriving at Tessa's gate, I stop and look up at the large mesquite tree on the other side of the fence. A flood of memories washes over me as I remember how Tessa and I would climb that tree. We'd spend hours up there—even hauling up snacks and drinks for the duration—spying on neighbors in their backyards and hiding from our parents when we were supposed to be working on chores. But mostly, we spent our time talking about boys and our future together. A future that no longer feels aligned and is more disjointed now than ever.

The shades of green and brown blur as I brush my cheeks roughly with my palms. I haven't even gone into the house yet, but I already feel a heavy weight bearing down on my heart, making it hard to draw in a full breath.

I've brought it on myself, though. I know better than to let my thoughts drift to those dark places and linger there. Blinking at the sun casting shards of light through the open branches, I take a moment to say a prayer. My words are lost in the breeze, and I can only hope they make it past the canopy of leaves and branches to their destination.

God, I need Your strength right now. For myself, and for Tessa. I

can't go in there carrying this burden. I'm supposed to be an encourage-
ment to her, Lord—a friend. Help me to shake off this gloom so I can
be strong for her.

Just as I finish praying, the front door swings open, and
Tessa's mom, Debbie, stands in the doorway. A long,
fringed blouse dotted with white flowers hangs low over her
faded jeans. She's barefoot, something I never remember
seeing before. Debbie always walked around the house in a
pair of fuzzy slippers or tennis shoes.

She has a puzzled look on her face, probably
wondering why I'm standing here staring up at the tree in
their front yard. I'd be confused too. I wave and open the
gate, hoping she doesn't question me about the tree-
gazing.

"Hey, Mrs. Williams! Did Tessa tell you I was coming?"

Her face breaks out with a big smile, and she reaches
out to hug me as I make my way up the porch steps. "Of
course, hon. And you know you're always welcome
anyway."

She looks good. She's missing that glow and the twinkle
in her eye that I've always admired about her, but she seems
to be feeling a whole lot better than she had a few months
ago. Not knowing where Tessa was and, like all of us,
bracing for the worst, Debbie had looked like a walking
corpse, barely existing day to day. That was on top of going
through a divorce from Tessa's dad a few months before
that.

This poor woman has had a really rough year, I think.

"Go on up, Alli. I'll give you guys a holler when dinner's ready," she says.

"Do you need help with anything?" I ask, glancing toward the kitchen, where the aroma of something delicious cooking drifts my way.

Resting her hand on my shoulder, she gives it a gentle nudge toward the stairs. "No, hon. I've got it covered. Tessa's expecting you."

I GLANCE at my watch and see that I've been sitting in Tessa's room for twelve minutes now. She knew I was on my way over.

Why didn't she take a shower earlier? I wonder.

I sit on her bed, playing a word game on my phone, listening for the water to shut off. The water's been running since I got here. Even I don't take that long in the shower, even though my dad always accuses me of using all the hot water.

I tire of the word game and start thumbing through posts on social media. I grin at a funny meme and admire a friend's post about her dog's new litter of puppies. They're Yorkshire Terriers. *I've been begging my parents forever for a Yorkie.* I start to send a personal message to my friend to ask about the puppies, then remember that I'm probably leaving for college and a dog would be pointless.

I hear the shower water turn off, and, a moment later,

the sound of metal scraping as the shower curtain is pulled back.

"Girls! Dinner's ready!" Debbie's voice echoes from the bottom of the stairs.

I scuttle over and crack open the door. "Tessa's just getting out of the shower," I call out. "We'll be down soon."

"Oh, okay," she says. "Tell her to hurry before the food gets cold."

I hear Tessa's brother, Aaron, rush past the room just as I close the door. His steps sound like a herd of elephants stampeding down the stairs.

"Alli? Is that you?" Tessa's voice is muffled behind the bathroom door.

"Yeah, your mom said that dinner's ready."

"K. Be right out."

Three minutes later, Tessa rushes out in a cloud of steam, and I get a whiff of her lilac-scented shampoo. Her oversized sweatshirt is damp from her freshly washed hair, and the bottom of her cotton shorts sticks to her legs where she must've just applied lotion. Walking over to her dresser, Tessa yanks open a top drawer. She mumbles something under her breath as she digs through it before jerking out a pair of socks. It's not until she plops down on the floor to pull them on that she even looks over at me.

"Hey." She sounds out of breath. "Sorry, I needed to shave my legs, and my hair was gross. Were you waiting long?"

I briefly wonder if she would think fifteen minutes is

long when you knew someone was waiting on you, but I push the thought aside. "Not too long," I say.

She doesn't answer but slips on the second sock and pops to her feet.

"Cool. Let's go eat. I'm starving."

Chapter Eight

AARON KEEPS US ALL LAUGHING AT THE DINNER TABLE. IN between mouthfuls of tater tots, he entertains us with a story about how his friend Ethan fell asleep in math class and was snoring into his backpack that he'd been using for a pillow. Aaron mimics snoring noises to complement his story.

"Mr. Grossman was oblivious," he says. "The guy's so old, he wouldn't even hear a bomb drop even if it was right in front of his desk. Anyhow, we couldn't stop laughing, and his face was turning beet red, and he was threatening us with detention because he thought we were laughing at *him*."

Aaron roars with laughter and Debbie and I join in. "Come on, really?" he continues. "How could he *not* hear Ethan snoring? Dude, it was more hilarious watching everyone try so hard not to bust out in hysterics. Lucky for me, I just shoved my face in my hoodie so Grossman couldn't hear me laughing."

Debbie and I crack up. I have to gulp down a sip of water so I don't choke on the bread I'm chewing.

"Why didn't someone just wake him up?" I ask.

Aaron shakes his head. "Nah, that would've spoiled the fun." I giggle and look over at Tessa, who's shaking her head and smiling over at Aaron. She's not laughing, but at least she's enjoying the story.

We had hamburgers and tater tots—deep fried instead of baked—for dinner. It's one of my favorite Williams family meals. I shove the last bite of my burger in my mouth and lick mustard off my fingers. My mom would be horrified if she saw me licking my fingers at the dinner table, but no one cares about those kinds of manners at the Williams' house. That's another reason I like coming here; I can defy the Mancini rules for a little while.

Pushing away from the table, I stand and start collecting plates. Debbie stands with me. "I've got it, Alli," she says.

I ignore her and continue clearing the table. Aaron slides his last tot through ketchup before tossing his napkin on his plate and pushing away from the table. I'm only mildly irritated that he never offers to help clean up because it's always been that way for as long as I've known Tessa's family.

Tessa stares down at the ice cubes floating in her tea, most of her burger and tater tots are left untouched on her plate.

"Are you done, Tessa?" I ask, reaching for her plate. Without answering, she rouses to help, standing and reaching for the empty glasses on the table.

The familiarity feels comforting as Debbie, Tessa, and I carry plates and glasses into the kitchen and drop them into the sink full of soapy water.

"How's your mom and dad, Alli?" Debbie asks, plunging her hands into the sink of bubbles. I finish scraping off a plate into the trash can and add it to the growing pile next to her. Tessa grabs a dishrag from the drawer, dips it in the soapy water, wrings it out, and heads for the dining room to wipe the table . . . all without saying a word.

I turn back to Debbie.

"They're doing good. Dad's out of town this week for a conference, and Mom has been teaching Avery how to use the sewing machine. She found a pattern for an apron in my Nonna Mancini's old chest in the attic and decided she wanted to try to make one for herself. It doesn't sound like it's going too well judging by all the complaining Avery's doing."

Debbie laughs and drops another dish into the soapy water. Realizing I'm standing here talking instead of help-ing, I turn the faucet on and start rinsing.

How long does it take Tessa to wipe a table off? I wonder, swishing water around a glass before setting it upside down on the drying mat.

"I took a sewing class in high school and hated every

minute of it," Debbie says. "I remember one of our assignments was to sew an apron, which is one of the easier projects we did that semester, and thinking that no one even uses aprons anymore. I even told the teacher that—I was a bit of a smart mouth back in those days—and suggested that she needed to update her old-fashioned pattern collection."

Debbie drops a handful of silverware on my side of the sink and continues. "She wasn't interested in my opinion and told me I'd make the apron if I cared anything about my grade. I ended up using the ugliest mint green fabric she had in her stash because I wasn't about to spend money for my own fabric to sew a stupid apron. My finished project looked like a kindergartner had pieced it together." She chuckles. "But my grandma saw that apron when I brought it home and loved it. She wore that hideous thing for years until it practically fell apart. I guess it proves that beauty is in the eye of the beholder, right?"

Debbie flicks soap off her fingers and leans over to rinse them. "Who knows, Avery might love it after it's finished."

There's something soothing about watching bubbles slide down glass and swirl into a white tornado down the drain. I wonder why I find it so captivating at someone else's house but couldn't care less about bubbles when I have to wash dishes at my own house.

"Well," I say, setting the last dish on the mat and drying my hands on a towel, "Avery and Mom went shopping for fabric, and Avery picked out a cute print. I have a feeling she's gonna want to keep the apron if she can just stop being impatient with the process."

Tessa shuffles in, shakes the crumbs off her rag into the trash, and drapes it over the edge of the sink to dry.

"Table's done, Mom. Come on, Alli," she says.

Debbie nods and takes the towel from me. "You go on, hon. Thanks girls."

Tessa's already at the bottom of the stairs by the time I trail after her. The walk up the stairs feels like a walk to a prison cell, and I find myself wishing I could've stayed in the kitchen and chatted with Tessa's mom instead.

I FIDGET by the door while Tessa moves things around on her desk and finally pulls out a large spiral-bound book. She tugs a desk drawer open and reaches in for a zippered cloth bag.

"Got any chocolate?" I ask, knowing Tessa always keeps stashes of candy bars and junk food hidden in drawers and odd places. Moving away from the door, I walk aimlessly toward the center of the room, unsure of where to park myself. I'm also curious about the book and cloth bag she's holding and what she and I are gonna do now that we're alone.

Tessa peers thoughtfully around the room, eyebrows scrunched as she considers my request. "Um, I think so."

She points to a wood box sitting on a shelf above her desk. "Yeah, see if there's anything in that box."

I walk over and slide the box off the shelf. I recognize it immediately and a rush of nostalgia washes over me like a tidal wave.

The box is long and crafted of solid wood with a small metal hook clasp in the front. It had once held ink bottles. One year, I think it was when we were in seventh grade, Tessa had been on a kick to learn calligraphy. We spent a whole summer spilling more ink than we used, learning to hold our cheap but impressive-looking fountain pens, researching the best nibs to use, and trying to master the art of angles and swoops to recreate the beautiful calligraphy of the woman in the YouTube video we'd watched at least a hundred times.

I was secretly relieved when Tessa finally gave up on the whole calligraphy obsession because I was never that interested anyway and had only joined in because Tessa talked me into it.

She was good at that—talking me into things—and, many times, that got me into more trouble than I'd like to admit.

Carefully lifting the lid, I notice that the ink bottles have been replaced by individually wrapped miniature chocolates in assorted flavors. I pick out several Dove milk chocolates and carefully re-clasp the lid before slipping it back onto its shelf. I peel the foil wrapping off a chocolate and pop it in my mouth.

"Yesss," I purr and smile over at Tessa, but she's at her desk, rummaging through the little cloth bag, and has her back to me. I shrug off the disappointment.

"Just what I needed. Thanks," I say.

Tessa glances over at me as she makes her way to the bed. "Oh, yeah, I thought I had some in there. Here, throw me one." She cups her hands together and holds them up for the toss.

I aim a chocolate at her cupped hands and miss. The chocolate drops on the bed next to her, and she scoops it up.

"Oh, hey, I almost forgot," I say. "You'll never guess what I found in my closet."

I walk over and grab my purse from the floor next to the bed. Reaching in, I pull out the gray hoodie and drop my purse back to the floor. I wave the surprise in my hands like a matador flagging down a bull.

Tessa looks up and grins. "I wondered where that went," she says and turns her attention back to the book on her lap. "You can toss it on my dresser. I doubt I'll ever wear it again anyway."

She sits in the middle of the bed, drawing in a large spiral sketchbook in her lap. I've never really known her to be interested in drawing, so it must be a new thing for her. I'm not brave enough to ask for a peek at what she's working on. Things still feel incredibly awkward between us, and each time we're alone in a room together, it feels like the ocean between us swells bigger and bigger, pulling us farther and farther from each other.

I think part of me was hoping that, by pulling out the forgotten hoodie and presenting it to her, the offering would spark some old memory that would coax us back onto common ground—or at least give us *something* to talk about that wouldn't feel like I was hijacking her privacy.

With Tessa being so absorbed in her drawing and me feeling like an unwelcome intruder, I lower myself onto a stool by the bed and attempt to distance myself and give her space.

I should just go home.

Squirming on the uncomfortable stool, I pass the minutes by peering around the room, absorbing the awkward silence with the mundane until I'm sure I'll just give in and come up with an excuse to leave early just to get relief.

The first thing I notice is the bareness of her bedroom walls. I try to remember what was on the walls before and am surprised that I've forgotten so quickly after being familiar with Tessa's room for so long. I remember that there used to be an Air Supply poster above her bed and one of Journey next to her dresser, but I don't see a trace of either poster now.

Oh, right . . . and all her animal posters. How could I forget?

Not the outdated adorable puppy and fluffy kitten posters of our elementary days, but huge, glossy posters of animal anatomy. Tessa had always talked about becoming a veterinarian after high school and started researching colleges back in our freshman year.

While Tessa poured over small animal pathology and canine behavior articles, I was still debating which faction I'd likely have been born into if I lived in the time of the dystopian *Divergent* book series. I concluded that I'd end up faction-less and be poverty-stricken for the rest of my existence just because I could never decide where I belonged in the world.

Tessa and I might've been bosom buddies, but there were times we existed on different mental planets.

Yeah, I was endowed with an active imagination while Tessa was gifted with a scholarly brain. That's what made us best friends: I kept her entertained with stories while she kept me motivated to pass my classes.

Bored with the bare walls and bygone memories, I turn my attention back to Tessa. "So what happened to all your wall posters?"

Pencil still in motion, she shrugs and says, "In the closet."

Oh, yeah, that makes perfect sense, I think, resisting the urge to roll my eyes.

When she doesn't offer anything more, I change the subject.

"Whatcha drawing?"

The pencil stops, and Tessa looks up at me with a vacant stare. "Do you *really* want to know or are you just trying to find something to talk about?"

Miffed, I throw my hands up. "Yeah, well, *someone* has to talk around here, Tessa. Help me out a little, will you?"

She tosses the pencil down on the book and slides both to the side, then plops her chin in her hands, resting her elbows on her knees. The expression on her face is coy and patronizing.

"Okay, fine. Talk," she says.

"I *have* been talking, Tessa. You just aren't listening. Would you rather I just left?"

I don't know what's come over me but I'm not feeling like walking on eggshells with Tessa right now. Maybe it's all the months of tense silence when there's a thousand unspoken words swirling around us that we're avoiding. At this point, the lines are blurred over who's avoiding the unspoken words more . . . me or Tessa.

Her patronizing stare shifts to seething anger. I'm kind of glad to see *some* kind of reaction from her—something to remind me that Tessa still has feelings somewhere behind her wall of indifference.

"I didn't ask you to come, Alli, and you are welcome to leave whenever you want!" She thrusts an upward-turned hand toward the door as she glares at me.

She's right. She didn't ask me to come. It was me who called her and asked if she cared if I came over. In fact, it's been me doing all the asking and reaching out since she came home from New Mexico.

No more. I'm done.

I'm like a stone as I stare back at her flushed face and

tight lips as it hits me that Tessa may never have needed, or wanted, me back in her life at all. That the ties had been severed so cleanly that there was no hope of reconnecting with her.

Up until now, I thought that Tessa's reservedness was just because she was hurting and had erected walls to protect herself. That all I needed to do was be patient and keep coming around, and she'd warm up and welcome me back with open arms.

Did I really believe that I was gonna swoop in and rescue her? Did Tessa even *want* to be rescued? By *anyone*?

Without saying a word, I spin around on the stool and reach for my purse, jerking it up to my shoulder. Pushing to my feet, I look down at Tessa still seated on the bed. Her eyes stay locked on me the whole time, the disgust on her face not diminishing one fraction.

I wonder why I've even bothered to keep coming back. Maybe I felt sorry for her. Maybe I felt guilty for my part in the whole mess. But I am washing my hands of it all—of *her*—tonight.

I don't say a word as I turn and walk out of the room, not even bothering to close the bedroom door behind me. Not once do I look back.

And Tessa doesn't call me back either. That hurts worse than anything.

Chapter Nine

My first period teacher, Mr. Ankor, is absent today, and, as luck would have it, there are no subs available.

There are *never* any subs available.

Depending on which teacher you eavesdrop on, the lack of subs is either due to severe district budget cuts or because the administration is too cheap to hire any. Either way, we have no teacher to replace Mr. Ankor this morning.

That means half the class is farmed out to Mrs. Phipps' room while the other half goes to Mr. Butcher's. I end up with the unfortunate group sent to Mrs. Phipps. She's the drill sergeant of the history department, and everyone—students and staff alike—is scared to death of her.

After we file into her classroom, she barks at us to stand up against the back wall like she's lining us up for a firing squad. Referring to an attendance sheet in her hand, she calls each of our last names alphabetically and thrusts a finger in the direction of the table where she wants us to sit.

Since her last name begins with a *B*, Shanice is one of the first names called.

"Shanice Bradshaw!" Mrs. Phipps snaps and points to a table at the back of the room.

Shanice saunters to the back corner table, snapping her gum loudly, and dumps her designer bag down on the table before dropping into her chair.

A few names later, Kim's name is called, and she's told to sit at a table near the door. Kim takes a few lagging steps in the direction of the table, then, with Mrs. Phipps' attention back on the attendance sheet, scoots around the edge of the room and slides into a seat next to Shanice.

When my name is finally called, I wince and stifle a groan when Mrs. Phipps points her dagger-like finger in the direction of Shanice and Kim's table. I briefly entertain the idea of pulling Kim's evasion trick and sneaking off to another table, but, as if she can read my mind, Mrs. Phipps actually stops to watch me walk to the table. As if I can't manage to find my way to the right seat.

I hear someone giggle next to me.

I hope you choke on your gum, Shanice.

I want to protest or at least point my own finger at Kim and announce, "Um, I think she's at the wrong table," but I know better. Shanice and Kim would get their revenge —somehow.

There's only one seat left at the table. Right next to Kim. *Yay, me.* I jerk my chair out and swing it away from Kim's and Shanice's uppity stares. I leave just enough of an angle for me to still use the table to write on.

Mrs. Phipps is already bellowing out more orders.

"Okay, everyone, listen up! Everyone is to pull out a sheet of paper and something to write with. I don't want to hear one peep from anyone, got it? I have my own students on top of all of you from Ankor's class, so I'm not in the mood for goofing off. Is that understood?"

She pauses and waits for our response. We hear a few mumbled "Yes, ma'ams" before she nods with satisfaction. She continues, "Okay. Get your supplies out, and I'll explain what we're doing as soon as I see that everyone's ready."

I focus on digging out a sheet of paper and a pencil. I set my pencil next to the lined paper and let my eyes roam around the room, focusing my attention on the parade of photos of former presidents neatly stapled across the top of the twin whiteboards at the front of the room.

My gaze wanders to the thousands of pin holes on the walls, where posters and decorations have been tacked to them and removed over the who-knows-how-many years that this classroom has been in use. Judging by the peeling salmon-colored paint on the walls, the classroom probably hasn't had an update since the early 70s.

I know it's not my imagination that at least two pairs of

eyes tunnel into me behind my back. And I don't *need* any imagination to know that Kim and Shanice are giving me their undivided attention. At this point, I'm seriously missing the boring worksheets Mr. Ankor makes us work on every morning. Anything would be better than spending a whole hour with these two making my life miserable.

When Mrs. Phipps turns around to write something on the board, a guy across the table from me mutters about how much he can't stand Mrs. Phipps and calls her some choice names. Everyone at the table either giggles or ignores him, all except for Kim. She gasps and I turn my head just in time to see her eyes widen and her fingers fly to her lips in obvious exaggeration.

"Colton, shame on you, you little sinner," she says, thrusting her thumb in my direction.

"*Sinner?*" Colton sneers. "Your mouth is way worse than —" Colton stops and follows Kim's thumb to me. "Who is *she?*" he asks, throwing Kim a dirty look.

Kim's jaw drops. "Surely you must know." She shakes her head in disbelief. "Oh, I guess not."

She leans forward, pulling everyone's attention to her.

"She's a *Christian*, Colton." Her voice purrs like a kitten, but her expression looks more like a lioness about to strike. "You can't talk like that around her or she might"—Kim turns her head to Shanice, who nods in perfect agreement with the direction Kim is taking this—"I don't know . . ." she says, her voice dropping to a whisper, "condemn your soul to hell."

Kim shoots a look at me like I'm a ghost she's come upon in a dark attic. The look I give her back probably makes everyone at the table wonder if she could be telling the truth about me condemning souls. But before I can spout off a snarky response, Mrs. Phipps marches over to our table.

Looking right at Kim, she says, "Perhaps you'd like to teach this class instead of me, young lady, since you have so much to say."

Everyone is staring at Kim, like vultures waiting for the death blow, hoping she'll accept the challenge and smart off to Mrs. Phipps and land herself in the office.

But Kim smiles sweetly and says, "No ma'am. Sorry."

You can almost feel the universal disappointment from the crowd. Mrs. Phipps moves back to the board, and I keep my gaze fixed on her for the remainder of the period. No one dares make another peep at our table, but I feel the disdain emanating from Kim as loudly as a trumpet blasting in my ear.

When it's time to pack up our things and Mrs. Phipps announces that we can chat for the last three minutes of class, Colton leans across the table.

"Hey, whatever your name is," he says. I know he's talking to me, but I ignore him and start shoving my things in my backpack. "Psst," I hear again. I jerk my head up and glare at him.

"What do you want?" I hiss, not caring who's watching the show at this point. I've spent the past forty-five minutes stewing over Kim making me look like a fool in front of the whole table for no reason.

If Colton plans to continue what Kim started, I'm here for it. I'm not backing down this time. But before Colton can answer, Kim jumps in, obviously determined to get back at me for her trouble with Mrs. Phipps.

"Chill out, church girl," she says. "And quit flirting with Colton. Didn't you learn your lesson after Chad?"

The sting hits its mark.

Colton's face melts into the background as images of Chad Barton flash through my head. The memory of how he used me for an elaborate prank and made me the laughingstock of West Morrison High School eclipses my view of Colton and everyone else surrounding me.

My hands tremble against my sides, and although I'm still glaring at Colton, my rage is now directed at Kim. I wasn't aware that the dismissal bell had rung until I see the other students start to file out of the room. But Kim and Shanice haven't moved from the table. They tower over me and clearly have no intention of leaving me alone just yet.

I don't know what to do. I'm so upset that I can hear the blood rushing in my ears and the top of my head feels like there's flames shooting out of it. When Colton pulls back from the table, it startles me, and I flinch. He looks at me, then looks away. Strolling over to Kim, he bumps his shoulder against her as he passes.

"Back off, Kim. Let's go. We're gonna be late."

I blink, fighting back tears, refusing to look up at Kim

or Shanice. After a moment, I sense them moving away. But I don't take my eyes off Colton as he walks away because I need something to focus on until I can reign in my emotions.

Just before Colton disappears through the door, he glances back and nods to me. There's a lift to one side of his mouth, like he'd smile if it wouldn't give away that he felt sorry for me.

My feet are cemented to the floor while my emotions scatter in a thousand directions. I feel like I'm flaking off in pieces like the hideous salmon-colored paint on the walls.

Why can't everyone just leave me alone? I scream inside. *As if they don't already have me labeled as a freak, now they're looking at me like I'm an unwanted dog someone left on the side of the road.*

But the look from Colton—that look of unsolicited compassion—undoes me enough that I have to race to the bathroom so I can burst out in tears in private.

Brynne tells me over lunch that Anthony had brought along a friend to the Bible study the other night.

"You know," she says, her eyes narrowing, "the Bible study where you dumped us to work on your *writing assignment?*"

I'm positive she has no clue that I made up that story to get out of a possible confrontation with Shanice, but the way Brynne says it makes me feel guilty all over again.

I think about the fact that Anthony invited a friend to join him and Brynne that night. I find it hilarious that he would go to such an extreme to avoid people thinking that he and Brynne are an item.

But, although I'm laughing on the inside, I secretly admire those qualities in Anthony: how he's so careful about everything he does and how he strives to have high morals. Anthony's not a puritan prude or anything, but he really cares about his influence as a Christian—even going out of his way to reach out to people and share his faith.

Anthony is everything I'm *not* in a Christian. I spend more time trying to dodge the issue of my faith than owning up to it, and I almost cringe when someone even brings it up. Without even trying, the walls go up, and I brace myself against misunderstanding and criticism.

I don't know why I feel this way either. It's just that I don't always want to talk about *why* I dress differently than others or *why* I can't go here or *why* I don't do that. Yet that seems to be all people want to discuss with me. It's never, "Hey, I admire the stand you take for your faith" or "There's something about you that I wish I could be more like."

No, it never happens like that for me.

It's not a question about if I love God, and I don't regret my decision to follow him, but I just can't handle being called out about about my faith constantly. Which is exactly what Shanice and Kim do every chance they get.

Like, even right now, as Brynne and I watch Shanice

approach while we eat our lunch. I feel a burning sensation churning in my stomach as I wonder why she's walking over here.

She's alone—surprisingly—trudging across the grass with obvious purpose, heading straight for Brynne and me as we sit at a table under our favorite oak tree.

"Oh, this should be interesting," Brynne says, snapping off the end of a celery stick and pointing it at Shanice.

"Is she seriously coming over here?" I ask.

She clearly is because there's nothing else out here besides an open area and the table we're sitting at. I doubt she plans on walking the track behind us.

"What does she want?" I scoff, and crumple up my empty chip bag in my fist.

She doesn't look at us, focusing instead on a building in the distance, until she's almost on us. Recognition flickers on her face, like she was out for an afternoon stroll and happened to run across us—which we both know isn't what happened. When she finally reaches us, Shanice ignores me and looks straight at Brynne.

"Mr. Stemms said he loaned you the quiz notes from Friday. Are you done with them?"

"Uh, yeah, he did. I'll give them to you next period." Brynne says.

Shanice shakes her head and nods toward Brynne's backpack. "I prefer them now."

Brynne looks confused but reaches for her backpack and pulls out the papers. She barely has time to offer them to Shanice when Shanice snatches them out of her hand.

"Thanks," Shanice says, tossing her long hair back and turning away. Brynne looks over at me wide-eyed, then back at Shanice's retreating back.

"I still don't get it, Shanice," Brynne calls out. "Why didn't you just get the notes from me later?"

Shanice barely glances over her shoulder and shrugs, never missing a step. "I didn't want to be seen talking to you," she says.

The look on Brynne's face is so comical that I can't help but burst out laughing. "Wow! Tell me that didn't just happen!" I say.

Brynne looks at me, to Shanice, and back to me, then starts laughing too.

"I do believe it did, my dear Sherlock," Brynne says, slapping a hand to her chest in feigned shock and tossing her curls back with a jerk of her head. "I didn't want to be seen talking to you!" she says mockingly, and we both explode with laughter.

I stand and throw my shoulders back, chin held high. I pick imaginary lint from my shirt sleeve and attempt to change my voice to sound like an arrogant lady with a British accent.

"Oh, no, my dear, I mustn't be seen engaging with you lest I taint my good reputation."

Brynne's face is laced with tears from laughing so hard.

We go on like this, playing off each other, until the bell rings, signaling the end of lunch.

For the first time, I feel like I have an ally who really gets what it's like to be scorned by the high-and-mighty Shanice.

Chapter Ten

I MISS BIBLE STUDY WITH BRYNNE AND ANTHONY AGAIN tonight, but my excuse is legit this time. Avery's sick, and my parents had a meeting they couldn't get out of. The lot fell on me to babysit.

Although Avery gets on my nerves like a sister, I'd do anything for her. Even stay home to be at her beck and call while she battles the stomach flu. You gotta love someone a whole lot to hold a trash can for them while they barf over the side of the bed.

I just hope I don't get sick next.

Mom and Dad felt really bad about leaving me home to play nursemaid to Avery but promised to only be gone an hour or two. After missing Bible study last week—which my parents have no clue about—I feel bad canceling on Brynne and Anthony again. But it works out that the friend

Anthony invited last Bible study had really enjoyed it and planned to go again tonight. At least it won't be just Anthony and Brynne alone.

After digging through the kitchen cabinets and finding an open sleeve of Ritz crackers, I pour half a cup of ginger ale and tear off a paper towel from the roll. Setting everything on a tray, I carry it into Avery's bedroom, which smells like sour milk despite the fact that I threw her barf bag in the outside garbage bin and doused her room with Lysol.

"Eww, you stink, Avery," I tease, setting the food tray down on her nightstand and grinning down at her pale face on the pillow.

Avery glowers at me from glassy eyes and moans. "It's not my fault, you know. Wait until it's your turn to be sick, and see how you smell."

I pull the desk chair close to the bed and fish out a cracker. Dangling it over her face, I say, "Maybe you wouldn't feel so bad if you didn't eat all those spicy chips. And . . ." I lift her hand from the blanket and hold it up to reveal the faint orange tinge of her fingertips. "Don't try to deny it. The evidence gives you away."

Jerking her hand back, Avery scowls. "That's not why I'm sick, Alli. I haven't had any real food since yesterday."

Pulling back in mock horror, I gasp, "And your fingers are still nasty? You haven't taken a shower since yesterday? That's just gross!"

Even though she giggles, I can see how miserable Avery is with her colorless cheeks and the dark circles cradling her eyes. I soften my tone. "It's alright, kiddo. Your secret's safe with me."

Holding the cracker to her lips, I encourage her to take a bite. She takes the cracker from me and sits up, nibbling on its edges. Then, she eyes the cup of clear, bubbly liquid. "What's that?"

Lifting it, I hold it out to her. "Ginger ale. Dad stopped by the store after work. Trust me, it does wonders for me when I have an upset stomach. Here, try it."

Avery takes the cup and looks between the cracker in one hand and the ginger ale in the other, her brows drawn tight. Her lips pucker with disgust.

"Go on," I say, nodding.

Taking a timid sip, she holds the fluid in her mouth for a moment before swallowing. "Not bad." She shrugs and leans back into her pillow.

Satisfied that the storm had passed for the moment, I stand and walk over to swipe my laptop from her dresser and plop down on a beanbag chair pushed into the corner of the room. I'm supposed to be defining economics vocabulary for an assignment due tomorrow but find myself opening a blank Google document instead. I feel the urge to try my hand at a creative story idea, something I rarely attempt.

She stood at the edge of the water, the surf washing over her feet before pulling back, a gentle tug to lure her closer ... deeper.

I type the sentence, then stare at it like I have no clue how it had gotten there. Yawning, I squirm deeper into my seat. My fingers rest again on the keyboard, but I'm not sure where I'm going with this story yet. The cushy beanbag chair is like a sedative that I can't fight, and my eyelids feel like they're weighted down with rocks. I look up at Avery and see that she's back under her blankets and her eyes are closed. I close mine too.

She digs her toes into the dense, wet sand and holds on. Glancing over her shoulder at the bleached expanse behind her, she feels a surge of warmth press against her back. A drowsy sensation floods through her, a tranquilizer lulling her to sleep.

Then, out of nowhere, an icy rush of air crashes against her chest, chilling her to the bone and sending shivers up her limbs. It wraps tight around her, pulling her down, down, down.

"Swim, Alli!"

She jerks at the sound of the voice, and the vortex of air recedes slightly but retains its grip. Swinging her head from side to side, she sees no one. The beach is deserted, except for three seagulls, which briefly pass overhead before they disappear into the misty fog of the open water. Her gaze trails along the miles of shoreline as far as the eye can see, then drifts over the bare sand behind her. Nothing. Had she imagined the voice? The swirl of icy air closes in again.

"Swim! Swim, child!"

Whirling around to locate the source, she loses her balance and tumbles backward into the rushing waves, her feet sucked deep into the wet sand. Before she can free herself, a wall of water washes over her, pinning her down. Sand and salt flood into her eyes and ears. She fights against it with all her might, but she can't move. She tries to relax—not fight against it—waiting for the tide to ebb and release her from its suffocating grip. But she panics instead.

As she struggles beneath its weight, the blanket of water grows heavier, completely engulfing her, the drenched sand beneath her dragging her down into its depths. From some faraway place in her conscience, she hears the voice—now fading to a whisper—compelling her to fight for her life .

I jerk awake, sucking in a great gasp of air, and notice one of my arms swinging wildly above my head. I pull the wild hand down and try to get my bearings.

What in the world?

It takes several deep breaths before I remember that I'm in Avery's bedroom. The room is darker now, but I can still make out Avery's form on the bed and hear the even breathing of her untroubled sleep.

My body trembles in the aftermath of the dream. Pushing myself up, I look around for my laptop, finding it open and resting sideways against the side of the beanbag chair. It must have slipped off my lap while I slept.

Okay, that was weird, I think, running a hand down my face, trying to clear the fog in my head. *Guess I won't feel much like going to the beach for a while.*

Pulling my laptop onto my knees, I save the document

containing the single sentence and push the laptop lid closed. I stand and tiptoe over to Avery, watching her in the waning light. The cup and crackers sit on the end table next to the bed, hardly touched. Avery sleeps peacefully, her color looking much better than it had earlier.

Gently tugging the door closed on my way out, I think about the dream. The details are already fading, but I can't shake the clarity of the voice still in my head telling me "Swim!"

"How's our patient doing?"

Mom sits on the couch across from me, heels kicked off and feet on the coffee table (usually a big "no-no" in the Mancini household), shoving pretzels in her mouth from an open bag on her lap. She and Dad had gone to dinner with an important vendor for Dad's computer tech company, and the vendor had taken them to a Chinese restaurant.

Mom hates Chinese food.

"Well, she only threw up twice and complained for the first hour, so I think Avery's gonna live," I say, snatching a pretzel out of the bag. "Want me to make you a sandwich or some mac 'n' cheese?"

Mom hands the pretzel bag over to me. "No, thanks, I'll grab a yogurt before bed." She stretches and pulls her feet from the table. "By the way, did you ever get the scholarship paperwork from your counselor?"

"Yeah, I did. I haven't done anything with it yet," I say.

"Shouldn't you have already started on all that? Don't you have to apply for scholarships before submitting college admission paperwork? I mean, you're almost done with school, and we have a lot of decisions to make if you want to start college next fall."

I study the pretzel in my hand and sigh. "I know. I should've had this stuff done months and months ago. Brynne's been on me about it too. It's just a lot to think about. There's so much going on with school, planning for graduation, church projects . . ."

I feel Mom staring at me and look at her. "I'm just making excuses, aren't I?"

We both laugh.

Grabbing her heels from the floor, Mom stands and looks down at me.

"Only you can answer that, Alli. But you can't avoid it forever. You're right—that paperwork should have been submitted long ago." Her face softens and she smiles. "Thanks for staying home with Avery and keeping an eye on her. I know you had to cancel your plans and I appreciate it."

I smile up at her and give a humble shrug, acting like having to stay home with Avery wasn't the perfect excuse for me to bow out of Bible study again.

"It's all good, Mom."

Rolling up the pretzel bag, I follow her into the kitchen

and put the bag in the pantry. "I'm gonna read for a while before bed," I say.

"Okay, sweetheart. I'm going to jump in the shower after Dad's out," Mom says.

"See you in the morning. Well, unless Avery infected me with her stomach virus and I end up barfing," I say. "In that case, I'll see you *before* morning."

Mom's chuckle fills the room before she strolls out.

Chapter Eleven

THE DREAM RETURNS AFTER I FALL BACK ASLEEP IN MY OWN room, but this time, the dream is fragmented and hazy.

The one detail that becomes clearer for me this time is the voice calling out for me to swim. I recognize the voice but can't place it. Even though I still feel the swirl of water engulfing me, I don't feel as panicked as I had in the first dream. A tranquility settles over me—a numbness that even fear doesn't seem to penetrate. A part of me even considers letting the water pull me deeper, leading me to places I've never explored before.

Then, a sudden urgency in the voice breaks through my conscience until it swells to a roar in my head.

"Fight it, Alli! Swim!"

I jolt upright awake. My body shivers under a thin layer of sweat on my skin.

"Nonna?"

I whisper into the dark room, trying to shake off the haze that lingers between the dream world and reality. The voice in my dream had been my Nonna Mancini's. But why? What did the dream mean?

I feel around for my covers and find them bunched at the end of the bed. I must have been thrashing about in my sleep and kicked them off. Tugging them up over my shoulders, I lie back down and think about the dream again, at least what I can remember of it.

When I was very small—maybe four or five—I remember having a terrifying nightmare while I was at my grandparents' house. Nonno Mancini was still alive back then. I was staying with them for a few days while my parents were out of town. I slept in the spare bedroom and remember waking up screaming in the dark room. Within moments, the hall light came on, and Nonno Mancini was standing over me, stroking my hair while Nonna stood behind him whispering, "It's okay, Allisandra. You're okay, tesoro."

I don't remember the dream, but I remember how Nonna's voice had calmed me that night. It continued to calm me throughout my formative years, well into my early teens, until God took her home to be with Nonno.

I could always talk about things with my nonna that I couldn't always share with my mom. It's not that Mom isn't a good listener. She always takes the time to listen and has great advice—and I guess I should tell her more often than

I do how much I appreciate that—but Mom is also a worrier.

She worried about me when things went south between Tessa and me, and I still see her concerned glances when she thinks I'm not looking. She worries about how I'll handle college and life away from home. If there's the slightest thing to worry about, Mom will find it and run with it.

Thankfully, Mom doesn't know about what happened with Chad and the times I went behind her and Dad's back. I'm not ready to admit all that yet either. Maybe when I'm older and our family is sitting around the table at Thanksgiving, sharing stories. That's the best time for grown children to confess to all the stunts they pulled as teenagers because parents can't do anything about the past. They just shake their heads in disbelief because everyone is supposed to be in a good mood for the holidays, right?

Anyhow, I see how Mom looks my way at the dinner table sometimes, or I catch her watching me from across the room, a pained look on her face. I guess it's just a mother's nature to worry all the time.

But Nonna Mancini never seemed to stress over things. Maybe moms outgrow the worrying when they get older, or they decide that we just have to figure things out for ourselves sometimes and let us have our space.

I don't know how that all works as we grow older. But I always felt like I could tell Nonna anything and she'd just take another sip of her coffee and say, "Tell me more about that, Alli." Or she'd click her tongue and nod her head while telling me, "Oh, mi cara, that must have been hard, but you're going to make it out all right."

But her voice in my dream had seemed urgent and so unlike my calm, unruffled Nonna. Was God using my connection with her to warn me about something important? Am I in danger of drowning emotionally, or does the dream mean something else? Or does it mean nothing at all and was just a bad dream?

God, are you trying to tell me something?

Chapter Twelve

N‌ow I know why everyone complains about Mondays being so awful.

Mr. Ankor is still out sick, and, yeah, I'm stuck at Shanice's and Kim's table in Mrs. Phipps' class again. However, it's just Kim today. Shanice is absent, but I almost wish she were here instead of Kim after Friday's humiliation.

Oh, and Colton is here too. Lucky me.

Colton banters back and forth with Kim and some other girl who moved to join our table. I notice Colton sneaking discreet peeks over at me with a look akin to pity or curiosity etched on his face. I also notice Kim and the other girl starting to look my way and not at all trying to be inconspicuous about it.

I'm not doing this again, I think and start looking around for an empty seat at another table.

I might ask Mrs. Phipps for a bathroom pass and hide

in a stall for the rest of the period. If anyone comes to check on me, I could always stick my finger down my throat and make myself throw up. Anything to get out of being trapped at this table for a whole hour.

Then a miracle happens—and it's definitely a miracle in my opinion. The phone rings, and Mrs. Phipps answers. She mutters a few words and looks toward our table.

Please, Lord, let the call be for me to go to the office or to inform me that my mom is picking me up and I'm leaving for the rest of the day.

But when Mrs. Phipps hangs up, it's Kim she's looking at instead of me.

"Kim, you're wanted in the counselor's office," she says.

Kim looks at the girl next to her and shrugs. Scooping up her notebook and backpack, she prances her way out of the classroom. With Kim gone, the other girl grabs her stuff and finds a new place to sit with one of her other friends.

That leaves just me and Colton. It's awkward, but anyone is better than Kim. Colton doesn't know me very well, and I'm not worried about him taking jabs at me without an audience around to egg him on.

I feel the tension drain from my body and pull out my laptop to start on the assignment written on the board, effectively shutting Colton out of my mind. The assignment is a website scavenger hunt for little-known facts about American history. I work my way through the assignment, which I find kind of fun, and am down to my last two history facts when I hear "Hey," from across the table.

Assuming Colton's talking to someone else, I ignore him. Until I hear, "Hey, church girl."

Yeah, he's talking to me.

Barely lifting my eyes to Colton, I grace him with my most scalding look and don't say a word, hoping to shut him up before he even gets started. He isn't intimidated one bit.

"Sorry, I don't remember your name." He grins. Then, seeing that I'm not amused, he tries again. "Okay, so you don't want to be called church girl. I get it. So what's your name again?"

"Alli." He's lucky I gave him that much.

"Alli. Got it."

Casting a quick glance at the door as if he expects Kim to come marching back in, he turns to me. There's a conspiratorial look in his eyes. "So what's Kim's and Shanice's problem with you? Was it because of that thing with Chad?"

With a sinking feeling, I realize that the "thing with Chad" is never gonna die and go away. Not while I'm at this high school anyway. I honestly have no idea what everyone heard about how things went down, but I can imagine the version Colton heard from Kim and Shanice.

There's no way I'm opening that Pandora's box with Colton. I don't want to know what he's heard, what he thinks, or what he'll run back and report to the others.

I raise my eyebrows and huff. "Good question. Maybe

you should ask Shanice and Kim because I'm oblivious to what their problem is."

I instantly regret answering Colton. For all I know, he could be messing with me just to get me riled up so I'll say something stupid. Then he'll use my words against me with them and start an all-out war. After trying for so long to lay low and stay off people's radar, I don't need the extra attention.

Nodding, Colton says, "Yeah, well, I'm in the dark too. In fact, that whole Chad thing was pretty messed up."

His eyes jump to mine. "I mean, I overheard some of the guys talking about it," he finishes lamely, catching sight of the dejected look on my face. I don't appreciate the reminder that I was the talk of the school for a while.

Mercifully, he changes the subject. "So you're a Christian?"

I'm caught off guard with the question. He'd obviously called me *church girl* for a reason.

I shrug. "Yeah, I guess."

I guess? Did I just say "I guess?"

I assume Colton doesn't notice the horrified look on my face because he nods like my answer is perfectly acceptable. Like sounding doubtful about what you believe and profess to follow isn't odd at all. I feel the need to correct myself.

I take a deep breath and start again.

"I mean, yes, I'm a Christian, but not like Kim and Shanice make me out to be. I don't belong to a cult, and

I'm not out there trying to preach about hell on street corners."

Which isn't exactly accurate because our youth group *has* handed out flyers on street corners, just not how Colton is probably picturing it. Realizing I'm digging myself further into a hole, especially with the puzzled look on Colton's face, I start to fidget with the pencil in my hand. I frantically search for a way to clarify what I said, but I'm not sure how. Before I can come up with anything, the bell rings, and Colton stands and grabs his backpack.

"That's cool," he says. "It would be kinda weird sitting at the same table with a snake charmer."

Colton laughs and swings his backpack over his shoulder. "Catch ya later, Alli."

Chapter Thirteen

"You really told him that you *guess* you're a Christian?" Brynne laughs at my explanation of the awkward conversation with Colton.

"Knock it off, Brynne. You weren't there . . ."

Resting a hand on my shoulder, she leans in close. "Well, I'm glad you made sure he knew you aren't in a cult. Think about it—"

"Brynne! You aren't helping at all. I was stuck in a bad place. I have no idea what Colton's heard about me. Did I mention that he brought the deal with Chad up? I felt like I should say something to defend myself. I wasn't expecting him to ask about me being a Christian. But then I felt like I needed to clarify and only made it worse. Argh, I'm so sick of this!"

To her credit, Brynne stops smiling and turns serious. She leans over to give me a hug.

"I get it, Alli. It's not like Colton didn't know you're a Christian—Kim made sure of that—but he put you on the spot. I'm sure he didn't mean to make it uncomfortable. He was probably just making conversation."

"Right, Brynne. Just trying to make conversation. He was probably seriously wondering if I really am a snake charmer."

My head falls back against the couch cushion. "Likely, he was trying to trap me into saying something stupid so he can blab it to Kim and Shanice."

Brynne looks amused. "Well, at least he'll be able to report back to them that you don't preach fire down on people from street corners. That's helpful," she says, giggling. "Oh, and that you are *definitely* not in a cult."

Before I know it, we're both laughing hysterically.

Brynne and I had been studying on the couch in her living room when she noticed how distracted I was. That's when I told her about my conversation with Colton. I'm glad I did too. Brynne is the best when it comes to giving advice. She's levelheaded and can usually talk sense into me when I'm acting dramatic.

I'm kinda surprised that she finds my conversation with Colton funny. But instead of being offended that she's not taking my dilemma seriously, I find myself feeling better just laughing about it with her. She's managed to pacify my anxiety and show me how I'm overthinking this.

"Hey, are you going to Anthony's surprise party this

weekend?" Brynne snaps her laptop closed, clearly through with studying and more interested in chatting.

Everyone loves Anthony, and I'm sure there won't be many who will miss this party. He has a reputation of being a really great guy whom everyone in our youth group looks up to and admires. He assists our youth leader, Brother McGuire, and it's basically accepted that he will be taking over when Brother McGuire steps down. Not that we expect that to happen any time soon. But if Brother McGuire hands the reigns to Anthony, we wouldn't want it any other way. That's just how much we respect Anthony's walk with God.

Pushing my own laptop to the side, I nod. "I'm definitely going. I gotta go shopping for a gift though, and I don't have any idea what to get him. What are you giving him?"

"I heard him say something about needing a new iPad case," Brynne says, "but I wouldn't know what he likes. Some of the other youth are putting together a gift basket for him and filling it with gift cards and snacks and stuff. Maybe we could just throw in something with that."

"Yeah, that sounds easy. I'll have my mom grab a gift card when she's out this week," I say.

Brynne has this mischievous look on her face but doesn't say anything. Of course, I know she expects me to ask.

"What? What are you thinking about?"

She shrugs and shakes her head. "Nothing. It was corny."

"*What?* Now you have to tell me, Brynne." Shifting my body to face her, I give her my full attention.

One side of her mouth lifts, and she wiggles her eyebrows. "I was thinking the perfect gift would be to arrange a blind date for Anthony for his birthday. Wouldn't that be a great surprise?"

I drop back against a pillow and shake my head.

"Whatever, Brynne. Just when I thought you had something interesting to say."

"Wellll, you have to admit, it would be fun to watch," Brynne says. "I mean, has the guy ever had a girlfriend in his entire life?"

I think about that for a second.

"Um, well, kind of. There was this one girl he met at youth camp one year who he seemed to like. I don't know if anything ever came of it."

Brynne throws her hands up. "When was that—when he was *twelve?* Come on, he's like twenty now, right? What's Anthony waiting for, Snow White to eat the poison apple or what?"

I snort. "Yeah, right. You can bet you'd never find Anthony kissing some strange girl he doesn't know."

"He's nineteen, Brynne," I continue. "And, if you're so worried about Anthony slipping into his golden years as an old bachelor, why don't *you* ask him on a date?"

Brynne cringes and puts a hand up.

"Whoa, let's not even go there. I don't have time to get distracted with some guy when I'm headed off to college, possibly in another state . . . like someone else I know." She leans in and pokes a finger into my shoulder.

"Yeah, I know. I'm working on it," I say.

Biting the edge of a thumbnail, I sigh deeply. "Are you . . ." I'm trying to think of the right way to ask this. "Are you gonna miss Tucson and us—I mean me and, you know, our youth group—when you go away to college? Do you ever feel scared or that you're not sure you are doing the right thing?"

All humor gone, Brynne wraps her arms around herself and stares down at the table. "Kind of. I know I'm following my heart, and I've prayed about it. There's a good church near the school, and Brother McGuire says they have a strong youth group, but, like you said, I'm gonna miss everyone here."

Brynne looks up at me with glistening eyes.

"But I'm really gonna miss you most of all, Alli. You're the one who first showed me about God and invited me to church. I'd feel so lost at school if you weren't there with me. What will I do without you in college?"

It's a good thing that it's just me and Brynne sitting in her living room right now because I hadn't planned on getting emotional. The tears come out of nowhere, and even though Brynne had been the one to turn the conversation, even she looks surprised to see me crying.

She scoots next to me on the couch and throws her

arms around me. "Oh, Alli, I'm sorry. I didn't mean to make you cry."

Brynne isn't crying yet, but I'm sure she's about to any second. Brushing a fist across my cheek, I pull myself together and slump back into the couch cushion.

"It's alright, Brynne. I don't think I'm only upset about leaving home and missing everyone. I think it's a bunch of other stuff too. I'm really nervous about going to USC and failing my classes—you know I'm not the best student—and what kind of roommate I might get stuck with. I really need to get a part-time job on top of my classes because I know I'm not gonna qualify for enough financial aid and my parents can't afford four years of college tuition. And . . ." I hadn't realized it was bothering me until just now. "I'm actually worried about leaving Tessa too."

Brynne gives me a puzzled look. "Tessa? Why would you worry about leaving Tessa?"

"I don't know, Brynne. I kinda feel like, well, I'm her only friend in the world."

Brynne nods. "From what you told me about your last visit with her, that doesn't seem to be accurate any longer," she says. "Do you even talk to her anymore? I mean, yeah, pray for her and all, but know when to take a hint that she doesn't want you around. Come on, Alli, you aren't Tessa's guardian angel or anything. I know it's been awful but, girl, you gotta stop dragging around guilt over what happened to her. You weren't the one who put Tessa in that situation."

I know she's right, but I still bristle at her words. How

can I expect Brynne to understand how I feel? Tessa and I had been like sisters growing up. Even though Tessa never shared my faith, it never seemed to be a big deal between us.

But I guess we couldn't put off the inevitable clash in morals forever. I was happy with the way things were, but I guess Tessa craved more excitement than what my friendship had to offer. Her need to try new things as well as her parents' divorce set her on a path that led her to places I don't think even Tessa really planned to go.

What eats at me now is that I can't help but feel I could've done more to help her. There's no one I can talk to about it either because, apparently, everyone has the same opinion as Brynne: Tessa made her own choices, and now she has to live with it.

No one has come right out and said that so bluntly, and everyone has shown nothing but concern and love for Tessa, but I still hear the verdict behind their words.

But I can't explain this to Brynne. I can't make her understand. I'd be wasting my time trying to explain it again when I've tried to do so a hundred times already.

"Yeah, I guess you're right." I sigh, burying my burden once again. "It's time to move on."

Brynne nods. "Yes, it is, Alli."

Grabbing my phone, I start scrolling, trying to appear to be looking for something when what I'm really doing is trying to avoid eye contact with Brynne.

"So," I say, staring down at my phone screen, "instead

of my mom buying a boring gift card, you wanna go shopping to get stuff to put in Anthony's basket this weekend? We could make it fun, like maybe buying a couple gag gifts to go with it. We just won't put our names on them."

Brynne's eyes light up, and I know we're back on safer ground. "Yeah, that sounds good. I need to shop for new shoes while we're at it. We can make a day of it."

Pulling my laptop closer, I'm ready to pull my focus back to studying.

"Cool. I'm sure I can find something I need to buy too. It's a date."

I turn my attention back to my screen, hoping Brynne doesn't try to continue our conversation about Tessa. When she picks up her phone and starts scrolling, I'm relieved.

I know she's right about moving on, but I'm just not sure if I know how to.

Chapter Fourteen

"Thanks for your help," Anthony says as I hand him the last folding chair to add to the stack against the wall.

The youth had organized a bake sale after the evening service to raise money for an upcoming youth trip. They'd worked really hard on decorating and baking and wrapping all the baked goods and had done a great job running the table, but, as is often the case, many hadn't stayed to clean up afterward. I'm sure Brother McGuire will have a few words to say about that at youth service this Friday night.

"No problem. I don't mind," I say.

Anthony leans the folding chair against the others in the stack and turns to me. "You heading home?"

I give him a puzzled look.

Where else would I be going at 9:30 on a school night?

But, of course, I don't say that.

"Yeah. Did you need help with something else?"

Looking around, I don't see anything left to do. When I turn back to Anthony, he's staring at me with an odd expression on his face that I can't interpret. After an uncomfortable silence, he shakes his head and glances around the room before turning back to me.

"No, we're good, thanks. Actually, I was wondering if . . ." He looks down at his watch. "Oh, maybe not." He looks up at me, then back at his watch, like he's not sure where to go from here.

"Wondering what?" I can't help but ask.

He lifts his head, but his eyes don't quite meet mine. He hitches one shoulder.

"Oh, I was just thinking that . . . well, we could go grab an ice cream or something," he says. He looks right at me now with an expression that begs me to rescue him, as if I could. "I mean," the words tumble out, "but, well, I didn't realize how late it was."

I don't know what to make of Anthony right now. First off, the whole youth group, including Anthony and me, have just ingested samples of fudge brownies and peanut butter cookies and everything else displayed on the tables tonight, and I couldn't imagine having any interest in ice cream after all that. But I'm starting to wonder if eating ice cream is even the point here. Maybe he's just not ready to call it a night and still wants to hang out.

"Uh, I guess it would be fun," I mumble.

I notice that there are only a handful of teenagers still hanging around. Most of the others have taken off already.

Turning back to Anthony, I say, "Want me to go see who all wants to go?"

Anthony just stands there blinking. His mouth opens, but no words come. I've never seen Anthony so flustered in all the years I've known him.

He must be in a sugar stupor or just exhausted from the long night, I think.

I'm just getting ready to start laughing and punch Anthony on the arm, telling him he'd be better off just going home instead of hanging out with the youth, when it hits me.

It's my turn to stand there blinking in shock.

"Oh, um, you didn't mean everyone? You meant just me and you?"

Anthony's cheeks turn bright pink, and he clears his throat—twice—before answering. Any other guy I know would have backpedaled and lied his way out of it, telling me that, no, of course he had meant for everyone to go— that not in a million years would he have meant just him and *me.*

But Anthony's integrity wins out—as it always does.

"Kinda." He stumbles over the word. "I mean, yeah, I was thinking just you and me could go. Together. You know, I mean, *of course,* us together. But then, I noticed what time it was and—"

He closes his eyes, shakes his head, and lets out a huff of air. When he opens his eyes to look back at me, he's got a huge grin on his face.

"I'm totally messing this up, huh?"

I don't need a mirror to know my cheeks are bright pink too. I can feel the heat on my skin so intensely that I'd gladly shove my head into a bucket of ice if there was one nearby. That would also give me something else to do besides squirm standing here in front of Anthony.

"I . . . uh, wow. Um, Anthony . . ." I blubber.

Anthony steps in with all the chivalry of a knight and saves me from my plight. Holding up a hand, he stops me from going on.

"Let's back up and try this again another time, okay? I know you need to get home, and I'm also aware that I completely caught you off guard. I'll go home and practice my lines, and maybe I can get them across more eloquently next time."

His teasing smile helps to ease the tension between us. But then he turns serious again. "That is, if you don't mind that there *is* a next time."

I've never been more grateful at that moment to see Blake heading our way, cradling a tall stack of decorations in his arms. Most likely, he's coming to ask Anthony where he wants them to be put away. Taking a deep breath, I give Anthony a timid smile.

"Yeah, sorry, you did throw me off guard. Maybe we better try this a different time."

Anthony's face softens. He takes a step forward, and my throat goes dry.

Oh, no. Oh, no . . .

"You got it," he whispers. "Until next time."

I've kicked off the blankets and pulled them back on so many times that I'll have to strip the bed in the morning and remake it because it's a crumpled mess.

My hand scans across the middle of the bed in search of my phone. I finally locate it under a pillow near the bottom of the bed. Pulling it toward me, I tap on it, realize I'm poking the back of the phone, and flip it over to hit the screen. It takes a second to adjust to the glare that assaults my vision as it lights up. I peer at the time: 2:48 a.m.

I'm never gonna make it through the day tomorrow.

Then, remembering that I also have to prepare for a presentation in my first period world history class—Mr. Ankor is feeling better and had hit the floor running with work for us—I drag the pillow over my face and groan.

Tossing the phone next to me on the sheet, I stare up at the ceiling and think of the reason why I haven't been able to sleep all night: Anthony.

What in the world happened with us last night? I think. *Did Anthony actually try to ask me on a date? First, I'm having freakish dreams about being sucked out into the ocean and my nonna calling out, and now I can't sleep because a guy I've known most of my life and someone I've idolized for years has suddenly shown interest in me.*

Reflecting over the past few weeks and months, I try to imagine any clues he'd given that he was interested in me that I had obviously somehow missed. I recall that, Sunday night, he'd held the door open for me as I walked into the church. Of course, he'd also held it open for Allison, so that cancels that out.

Did he smile at me but not at Allison though?

When Anthony led prayer during youth service, had he purposely locked eyes with me after saying "amen," or am I imagining that?

Yeah, I'm probably imaging that.

Oh, stop it! I chastise myself.

I can't deny the obvious fact that Anthony asked me on a date. Well, a prelude to a date since he'd only suggested getting ice cream. That's not a real date, right? It's not like he'd suggested a five-star restaurant with real cloth napkins and water served in wine glasses. But, even going for ice cream tonight would've still been just the two of us. Alone.

Yeah, I'd classify that as a legit date.

Right? I groan out loud again. *Why am I so clueless about this kind of stuff?*

I'm not sure how I feel about all this either. I mean, do I even *want* to go out with Anthony? Do I feel anything for him outside of my admiration of him in every way? Am I *supposed* to feel anything right now, or does that come later?

Sure, I've always considered Anthony good-looking and appreciate how responsible he is and that he has high morals. But is that just admiration, or could I ever be into him, as in, like, a *boyfriend?*

I know I'm overthinking this, I overthink everything.

Wow, I'm starting to act like Mom.

Goodness, the guy only asked if I wanted to go for ice cream, not design wedding invitations. Becoming his girlfriend had never been mentioned. But Anthony had to feel some kind of attraction to me. Why else would he have asked?

I lean over and tap my phone again. *3:06 a.m.*

Screwing my eyes shut, I snatch back the pillow and bury my head under it, hoping I'll get at least a few hours of decent sleep before my alarm goes off.

It's not looking good though.

Chapter Fifteen

SHE'S THE LAST PERSON I WANT TO SEE WHEN I COME OUT of the bathroom stall, but it's not like I can do anything about it. It *is* a school bathroom, and she has as much of a right to be here as I do.

We don't acknowledge each other even though I have no choice but to wash my hands at the sink next to her—it's the only other sink in the room.

When I look up to check my hair in the mirror, our eyes meet. Her eyes are puffy and red, and she looks like she's one stone away from the whole dam collapsing.

"Shanice? Are you okay?"

She doesn't answer but drops her eyes and flicks water off her fingers into the sink before reaching over and yanking a paper towel from the dispenser on the wall. I pretend to keep washing my hands because I feel stupid now. I had obviously caught her in an embarrassing moment, and now she'll probably despise me even more than she already does.

Whatever.

I stall as long as I can before turning the water off and waiting for Shanice to move aside so I can reach for a paper towel. I consider drying my hands on my skirt to be done with it so I can move on, but I wait. However, instead of moving out of the way, Shanice reaches up and pulls a paper towel out and hands it to me.

"Thanks," I say, quickly taking it from her like I'm afraid she's gonna stuff it down my throat if I'm not fast enough. I don't dare look at her again, but I hear her sniff and clear her throat.

"No. I'm not okay."

I lift my eyes to look at her, face-to-face this time instead of an image reflected in the mirror. Her face is pale with patches of red blotches, and her mascara is smudged on one eye where it looks like she tried to do damage control and failed. There's a long strand of dark hair plastered against her damp cheek and a lipstick stain on her white crop top. I've never seen Shanice look anything but put together. Her hair and makeup are always flawless.

Whatever she's upset about must be pretty bad.

Shanice looks like she's about to say something but then seems to decide against it. A thousand thoughts fire off in my head while I weigh whether to let the moment go or swallow my pride and encourage her to open up. Before I can make a decision though, Shanice brushes past me and out the door, the brief moment gone.

I stare down at the towel in my hand like I've forgotten its purpose.

What in the world just happened?

Coming to my senses, I dry my hands and toss the towel in the trash. I make my way back to class but can't remember much else about what we worked on for the rest of the period. When Brynne catches me in the hallway after class, her face is a puzzle of concern.

"Don't tell me you failed the economics test."

It's my turn to look puzzled. "What? No. The economics test is next week."

I tug Brynne along with me toward my sixth period class. Leaning close, I whisper, "I just had the weirdest thing happen in the bathroom."

Brynne stops and stares wide-eyed at me. "Whoa, do I *really* need to hear this?"

Rolling my eyes, I grab her arm and push her forward. "Keep walking. I don't want to make it obvious."

I look over my shoulder just to make sure we aren't drawing too much attention and to confirm that Shanice isn't in sight.

Brynne leans close and says, "News alert, Alli. We *totally* look suspicious. Hurry up and tell me what happened already. You're freaking me out. Was someone smoking in the bathroom again?"

"Noooo." I give her a pointed look. "That's nothing

new, Brynne. There's *always* someone smoking in the bath-room." I lean in and whisper, "I ran into Shanice in the bathroom, and, get this—"

"What's up, Brynne!"

Brynne spins around and waves to her friend, Chris, who jogs up and gives her a fist bump before moving on. "See ya, Chris!" She calls out before turning back to me.

"*And?*" Brynne says. "What's the big deal with running into Shanice? Did she say something to you? What happened?"

We're in front of my journalism class, and the bell is about to ring. I don't want to make Brynne late for her next class.

"I'll talk to you after school. Are you still coming over?" I ask.

Her jaw drops. "You're kidding me. You're just gonna leave me hanging like that?"

"I know, sorry," I say. "We don't have enough time to talk. So are you still coming over?"

"Yeah," she sighs. "Meet me in the parking lot. We'll grab some snacks at the gas station and talk on the way to your place. I can't wait to hear this, Alli. Bye!" She turns and sprints down the hall.

Yeah, you are definitely gonna want to hear this, I think.

~

I'VE BEEN STARING at the article I'm working on about Brynne for ten minutes with no progress.

Scott, the editor for our school newspaper, has walked by at least five times with a concerned look on his face. I know he's dying to ask how the project is going and offer his input because that's just how he is. Scott is a great editor, but he can be a bit of a micromanager. I'm sure the only reason he hasn't already poked his nose over here is because I throw him a dirty look every time he passes.

Even Scott knows when to back off.

I've read the article at least ten times, and it still sounds, well, uninspiring. No one really cares about the valedictorian's grades and her lofty ambitions for college. Yeah, Mr. Porter, my journalism teacher, expects those details to be included, and I've got them down, but I'm beating my head against the wall trying to make the article more interesting.

I want the piece to give readers more insight into who Brynne is as a person: where she wants to be in five years, her hobbies, or what her favorite food is (I discovered it's veal parmigiana because she literally freaked out when I mentioned that my dad was making it for dinner one night. Naturally, I invited her for over.).

Realizing that staring at my computer screen is not increasing my word count for this article, I save it and tab over to see if there's something I want to buy from my Amazon Wish List. I'll just have to sit down with Brynne and dig up some more interesting facts on her later.

Two new paperback books and a phone case later, I

snap the laptop closed and set it to the side. I scroll through photos on my phone and see the one of Brynne and me posing in front of her house after we'd just got done washing her car, which had led to us torching each other with the hose. We look like drowned rats in the photo, but our smiles reveal that we hadn't minded a bit.

That's the best part of hanging out with Brynne—you never knew what crazy thing she might come up with. And without Tessa around at school, I'm thankful to have someone like Brynne to hang out with every day.

Thoughts about Brynne and school bring up the memory of Shanice and our brief and very awkward meeting in the bathroom.

I can't stand to be in the same universe, much less the same room, as Shanice. She's been a thorn in my side for most of this school year. That's just one of the many reasons why I'm glad we're seniors. Shanice Bradshaw and her shadow, Kim, will both be out of my life as soon as we flip our graduation caps to the sky.

After Tessa made the cheer team and decided that I was no longer best-friend material, it's been nothing but one irritation after another for me. Kim and Shanice decided to zero in on me and, every chance they got, made snide remarks about how I dress, my religion, and whatever else popped into their snobby heads to spout about. I've never had people who hardly even know me despise me so deeply.

There's a lot of reasons I can't stand Shanice.

But there was something—I don't know—*vulnerable*

about Shanice when we met in the bathroom today. It was like I had a small peek behind the mask she keeps in place for the world and saw another side of Shanice that I didn't know even existed.

For once, there was no smirk on her face or any smart comments rolling off her tongue. She looked lost and fragile. It wasn't because she didn't have her girlfriends around for an audience either. Shanice could be just as obnoxious on her own, without help from friends, so there had to be another reason why she'd looked so vulnerable today.

I wanted to feel superior in that moment and take advantage of the rare occasion to pick at her wound for a change. Part of me wanted to point my finger right in her face and say, "How does it feel to be human like the rest of us, Shanice?"

But I couldn't conjure up the motivation to do it, whether or not I felt she deserved it. For one thing, I know that it wouldn't be pleasing to God for me to retaliate. And, two, I don't have the capacity to be that cruel, no matter what she's put me through in the past. My opinion doesn't matter to Shanice anyway.

Besides, I don't want to start acting like . . . *her.*

I can't explain why, because Shanice doesn't deserve one ounce of my pity, but I feel bad seeing her like that. On the other hand, it almost makes me mad to see Shanice out of her mean-girl role.

I don't appreciate the tables being flipped on our roles and throwing me out of whack. The Joker and Batman come to mind. Everyone expects the Joker to be Batman's nemesis. Batman would *never* catch the Joker crying in a bathroom and feel like he should say a comforting word or pretend to care. That would mess with our heads. Just as seeing Shanice being fragile is messing with mine.

Which is also why I'm not sure I feel good about sharing the whole thing with Brynne now. As much as I'd like to expose Shanice's weak moment and even relish in it, the thought doesn't settle well with me.

Okay, God. I get it. I should take the high road here and leave it alone.

But Brynne is gonna ask me when I see her after school. What am I supposed to tell her now?

Chapter Sixteen

OF COURSE, BRYNNE HAD WANTED THE SCOOP ON SHANICE the minute we met up after school.

I really wanted to tell her every detail about the bathroom scene, but, well, it just didn't feel like the right time. I actually told her that too. She was gracious about it, but I know telling her that only served to stir up her curiosity even more. She gave me suspicious looks the rest of the ride home as if she thought my sanity might be in question.

I'm heading to the school library when I hear someone behind me in the hall.

"Hey, church girl!"

I recognize the voice right away, and it makes me mad.

"You can quit calling me *church girl* because you know my name—"

I spin around to face Colton and put a stop to his irritating jabs when I come face to face with Chad Barton. The guy who'd all but destroyed my reputation and my ability to show my face in the halls of West Morrison ever again.

Chad looks just as shell-shocked as I feel, with eyes wide and unblinking, a flush of pink crawling up his neck. Somehow, in the moment, I still have my wits about me enough to recognize that Chad is blushing. Either that, or it's a rash he's suddenly developed being in my presence.

Maybe both.

Colton is standing next to him and looks at me and then at Chad, following the invisible tension line between us, a puzzled look on his face. I glance at Colton and back to Chad, my body a tangled mass of nerves. When Colton forces a cough, I know that how uncomfortable the whole situation just became has hit him and he's probably trying to work out an escape plan.

"Oh . . ." he says, the word dying on his lips. "Uh, hey . . . Alli."

I feel more than see the subtle shift of his body moving forward as Colton attempts to break the spell and insert himself between Chad and me. He knows about everything —well, maybe not *everything*—that went down with Chad's cruel prank and how he'd played me for his friends' entertainment.

But he probably wasn't remembering all that when he called me out just now with Chad walking beside him. I can't blame Colton for forgetting, but I do resent him for it.

"What's up, Alli?" Chad manages, a slight lift of his chin that borders on the line of friendly.

I don't take the bait.

Turning to Colton, I can't quite manage a smile. "Hey, Colton."

"I was teasing about the church girl thing . . . just rattling your cage," Colton says, his voice slightly strained.

He keeps his foot between Chad and me, but his posture is more relaxed. My gaze flickers over to Chad in what I hope looks like well-deserved irritation before I adjust my backpack on my shoulder and turn away. I'm not even gonna acknowledge Colton's comment. The last thing I want is to draw more attention to myself.

What I'd love to do instead is to melt into the air vent on the floor a few feet away. My skin is already prickling with anxiety over them watching me walk away.

"Catch you, later," I say over my shoulder, deliberately snubbing Chad. Every pore in my body dares him to say a word.

Just one word.

To my relief, he doesn't. Colton doesn't reply either. I have no choice but to start walking, knowing they are watching, probably snickering and sharing snide comments about me as I go. But the farther I get, the better I feel.

I'm not the fangirl of Chad Barton that I once was. I'd blown him off and shown him that he had no power over how I feel anymore.

I'm super proud of myself for it too.

∾

When Chad Barton broke my heart, I had been starstruck and vulnerable. Vulnerable because Tessa had turned her back on me in favor of acceptance and popularity. I was hurt, devastated, crushed.

It's already hard enough sticking out like a sore thumb compared to other girls at school. Wearing dresses, having long hair, not wearing makeup—that makes me stand out.

It's something I really struggled with—*still* struggle with.

I don't like being different. I mean, I don't really mind the fact that I don't go with the crowd and choose to steer clear of the not-so-good stuff. I've never been into partying and having a foul mouth. But it's the looking-different part that rubs a raw part of me for some reason.

Maybe it's because I'm seventeen and most seventeen-year-old girls don't want to be labeled as being "different" because they're afraid that they'll be branded a weirdo because of it.

But Chad took it to a whole new painful level when he made a public show of seducing the "Christian girl" to see how far he could drag me along before I figured it out. And I went along just fine, feeling like I was up there on the same level as all the gorgeous, popular girls and that other girls envied Chad's attraction to me.

What was I thinking?

The only redeeming positive fragment that I discovered in the aftermath was that Tessa wasn't part of the whole plan. At least that's what she told me, and I believed her. I still do.

Tessa.

I miss the Tessa I knew so much. Her glory days of cheer and hanging with the in-crowd are over, and all that's left is a mere shell of the best friend I'd known.

Where does that leave me? Could my own poor decisions have led me down the same path? How was I any different than Tessa if I was willing to compromise my standards in order to feel better about myself and gain the attention of someone I thought would improve my position on the social ladder?

I'm far from the model Christian girl that others, including my own parents, think I am.

But I can't fool God. He knows my heart better than anyone else. I know I'm lacking in a lot of areas, but I try to read my Bible most days and say quick prayers throughout the day. But I'm not as committed to my faith as I'd like to be. Sometimes it feels like I'm just going through the motions and my heart's not in it.

Why does everything have to feel so hard?

My dream.

I think about the dream that I had about the voice telling me to swim when I felt like I was being pulled under by water—the voice I thought sounded a lot like my Nonna Mancini.

The dream haunted me for a few days, and I couldn't put it out of my mind. I didn't understand what it meant— if anything. As they say, it was just . . . a dream. But, just maybe, I was working through something in my subconscious.

I *have* felt overwhelmed lately with decisions I need to make and not having clear direction about what to do with my life. Sometimes, it *does* feel like I'm drowning under the burden of it all, and it would be just like my nonna to step into my dream to offer a word of encouragement—or warning.

My shoulders slump as I exhale all the air in my lungs. Defeat hangs over me like a threatening cloud.

I tell myself that all will be better when I move to California and have a new start.

But, if I'm honest with myself, that's not likely to happen. Like my mom tells me, I have to settle things in my mind and in my heart *before* I move on because adversities will follow me wherever I go.

And one of the issues I know I have to come to terms with is forgiving Chad Barton. I'm the one still carrying around the baggage of anger and bitterness. It's not like he loses sleep over what happened.

Chad Barton doesn't need my forgiveness—he probably couldn't care less—but I need the peace that comes with forgiving.

I feel a tug on my heart and recognize it for what it is: God's still, small voice.

I know that forgiving Kim and Shanice are just as important as forgiving Chad, but I'm not ready yet. Forgiveness for them isn't even on the horizon right now.

Maybe it's because Kim and Shanice pick the scab on our relationship on a daily basis, while there's some distance between what happened with Chad.

Most days, I'm closer to punching Kim and Shanice in the face than offering forgiveness.

And that's nowhere close to the attitude a Christian girl should have.

Chapter Seventeen

"Hey, church girl, you got any extra paper?"

I don't need to turn around to see who's asking, knowing that Colton is just pushing my buttons again. I flip to the back of my binder and tear out a blank sheet of lined paper. Turning, I dangle the paper above his open hand.

"It's Alli—not *church girl*—remember?" I hiss.

"Oh, right. So *snake charmer* would be out too?"

He's smiling, so I know he's just poking at me, but I still throw him a dirty look. "I wouldn't if I were you," I say, "unless you want me to call down fire from the heavens and burn you to a crisp."

He laughs and writes his name at the top of the paper.

Satisfied, I turn back around and start copying the notes Mr. Ankor has written on the board. Even with all the catch up work he's making us do after his absence, I'm relieved to have our teacher back, with Mrs. Phipps and her seating arrangement a bad memory I'm eager to leave behind.

Colton's not a bad guy, now that I've gotten to know him better. He acts a little distant when Kim's around—and, thankfully, she's sitting across the room now—but he doesn't join in when Kim targets me for some spiteful remark or makes me the target of her jokes. I appreciate that small act of kindness from him.

What I haven't been able to figure out is that Shanice has been sitting alone at a desk close to Mr. Ankor's this whole week. Colton doesn't even ask Kim why, and I assume that's because he falls into the everyone-knows-except-for-Alli-Mancini category.

However, when I look for her this morning—*why am I looking for Shanice?*—I notice that Shanice's desk is empty. A quick peek around the room reveals that she's not in the room at all.

Huh, I think. *She must be absent. And . . . who cares?*

I drag my focus back to my work so I don't get stuck with homework again tonight. I'm so engrossed in copying down vocabulary definitions that I'm surprised when the dismissal bell rings. Looking around, I see that most of the students already have their things packed up and are huddled near the door. Even Colton managed to slip out from behind me without me even noticing. I throw my stuff in my backpack and make a dash for the exit.

I'm almost to the door when I hear a voice—*her* voice—close behind me.

"Hey, Mrs. Puritan," the voice hisses. "I heard Brynne is trying to recruit Shanice into your little cult. You better keep an eye on Shanice, especially around those innocent church boys. You can't trust her."

I swing around to face Kim, seething on the inside. The smirk on her face tells me that she's ready for a fight, one that she knows she'll always win and that I'll always be on the losing end of, no matter how hard I try.

Her condescending look that takes me in from top to bottom reveals how unworthy she thinks I am to be anything more than a pincushion for every stab she wants to thrust in me.

But what Kim doesn't know is that I don't care what she thinks, that I've never cared, and that I never *will* care. And, although looking different and being different doesn't come easy for me, if I wanted to be like anyone, it would never be like her or her kind.

That knowledge gives me the courage to stare directly in her eyes and smirk right back. I know it's not very Christian of me, but my faith doesn't make me a doormat either.

"I have no clue what you're talking about, and I don't care either. Shanice might not realize it, Kim, but she's a hundred percent better off without you. You leave an ugly smudge on every person who gets anywhere near you. It's *you* I wouldn't trust. And any one of our 'church boys' would see right through you in a second, so back off."

Thrusting my chin in the air, I brush past her, purposely swinging my backpack in her direction, satisfied when it makes contact with her shoulder and nudges her off balance.

Walking full speed ahead, I don't give Kim a chance to respond.

I'm close to the door when I notice Colton standing there. I know he's seen and heard the whole confrontation.

"I don't want to hear one word," I say, my chin lifting high in the air as I breeze past him and out the door.

I'M NOT sure where all this bravery has come from lately.

Putting Kim in her place—although I doubt she'll stay there—and snubbing Chad. Sure, at the time, I was proud of how I hadn't given Chad the satisfaction of me acknowledging him, but now I feel sort of dumb. And immature.

But the things I said to Kim, well, she needed to hear them, and I don't regret it.

Sorry, God. I couldn't resist. I know you're disappointed in me and that you expect me to take the high road and forgive my enemies. Does it count that I didn't unload on Chad like I did with Kim? One better choice out of two isn't too bad, right?

I know God isn't standing over me with a bat, ready to strike a blow to the back of my head for every infraction, but I still feel like a scolded puppy. It's the same way I feel when my parents come down on me after I fail them, only for them to remind me afterward how much they love me and that they're still proud of me. I always feel worse after that.

Like I feel right now.

Suddenly, my bravery feels more like the cheap way out. It's not that I believe that I'm required to take every abuse that's dished out and that I can never speak my mind. It's more about what I've really gained in how I handled both situations. Did it make the situation better or just make me feel better?

God, what am I supposed to do with all this? Kim . . . Shanice . . . Chad . . . Tessa? I feel like I'm spinning in an emotional tornado, being hit with debris from every side. It doesn't affect Brynne like it does me. She doesn't have as much invested as I do—or as much to lose. To be honest, I feel like I'm maneuvering through this alone. The choice to be the better person, to be strong for others when I don't want to—that feels unfair.

Tessa is a broken vessel that doesn't have the capacity to carry any of my feelings if I were to share them with her—where I was left after she walked away from our friendship or how I felt in the aftermath of Chad. While I'm glad that Tessa has a tribe around her for emotional and mental support, where was all that when I needed it—still need it?

I stare down at the coffee cup in my hand.

It's an old, yellow ceramic mug with a chip along the rim that I always have to remind myself to avoid when I drink from it. But it's my favorite cup because it was my Nonna Mancini's. She and I always used to sit on the porch and talk about life. Of course, my life was much different back then, before Nonna passed, than it is now. I wish God would loan Nonna back to me for at least an hour or two so we could have one of our chats on the porch again. I know it would help. It always did.

But we don't always get what we want in life. Sometimes we have to figure it out for ourselves. Not that God doesn't give us a hand, but, sometimes, he's a lot slower answering than I'd like him to be.

Is going off to college a good idea? Is it time to just write Tessa off as a loss? Do I just tolerate the morons at school until I get to be rid of them after graduation? Do I explore the possibility of something between Anthony and me?

Until God either writes the answers on the wall or makes it clear enough for me to understand, I'll just have to figure it out on my own.

Just little solitary me.

Flying solo.

Hoping I don't have a crash landing.

Chapter Eighteen

It couldn't be avoided.

I knew I'd have to tell Brynne about my run-in with Shanice eventually. I couldn't stall forever. But I plan to keep my confrontations with Kim and Chad to myself for now because I only have the emotional stamina to work through one drama at a time.

Brynne and I are draped across a large wooden bench on her back porch, where we've been scrolling through Pinterest, pinning hairstyle and fashion inspirations that we'll likely never use.

It's when she scrolls to a photo of a girl with long, glossy brown hair and piercing dark eyes who looks like a dead ringer for Shanice that the topic resurfaces. Brynne doesn't even have to say anything. She just points at the photo and rolls her eyes over to me.

I push myself up and sit cross-legged, facing her on the

bench. Tucking the phone under her hip, she slips her hands behind her head and gives me her full attention.

But when I start to tell Brynne the story, I end up downplaying the bathroom scene with Shanice so much—maybe too much—saying only that Shanice *seemed* upset and looked like she *might* have been crying, that Brynne loses interest after a minute.

In fact, after all the suspense I'd put her through waiting for me to fill her in, I detect the disappointment on her face. I expect her to spout off with "That's it? You made me wait for *this*?"

"Well, maybe she really does have feelings under that hard exterior," was her dismissive response.

That was my out.

I could've and *should've* moved on and dropped the subject since that's what I knew was for the best anyway. But I find myself holding on to it, keeping my grip on the conversation as if there are words left unsaid that need to be expressed.

"I think she does," I say.

Then, seeing the mask of confusion on Brynne's face, I add, "Shanice. I mean, I think there really is something under all that rudeness and sarcasm."

Brynne's brows lift, urging me to go on. She's probably wondering what spurred my melancholic reaction and where I'm going with this.

I don't know, maybe I'm feeling a bit melancholic and reflective at the moment. Or maybe I'm still in shock that I had been gifted a rare view into the human side of Shanice and am having a hard time believing it myself.

"Stop looking at me like I've just stepped off the crazy bus. Hear me out."

She lifts a hand and rolls it forward in the air, encouraging me.

"What do you think makes Shanice so . . ." The fitting word I'm looking for doesn't materialize. "Prickly?"

A single snort, which I assume is a failed laugh, bursts from Brynne. "*Prickly?*" she says, now full-on giggling. "That's an interesting description."

I try to hold back the eye roll but don't quite manage it. "Grouchy, rude, obnoxious, snotty . . . you know what I mean."

Biting down on her lip, Brynne sits up and folds her legs under her, facing me, as if pulling herself together and attempting to align herself with my mood.

I can feel the well-meaning advice coming.

"I don't know, Alli. What makes anyone the way they are? Think about it for a second. Shanice hangs out with Kim and those other girls. That should explain a lot right there. You know the proverbial 'great minds' think alike." She uses air quotes to emphasize the intended sarcasm. "And, let's be honest, cheerleaders are just stereotypically snobs."

She shoots a palm up. "Not my rule—just how it is."

Neither of us speak for a moment. We just sit quietly with our thoughts. From a nearby yard, there's the sound of a sliding door opening and closing, then there's a wail from a baby a few houses down.

Brynne scoots herself back on the bench to lean against a concrete post. She hugs her arms across her chest, a thoughtful look on her face.

"You know," she says, "I think that it's also possible that Shanice doesn't feel too great about herself. You know how the saying goes: People who don't like themselves, don't like anyone else either."

I nod, thankful that the conversation has taken a more serious tone.

"It makes me curious if Shanice has always been so offensive," I say, "or if she started acting that way after she joined the cheer team like—"

"—Like Tessa," Brynne says, finishing my thought.

"Yeah," I sigh. "Like Tessa. Seriously, I've been friends with a lot of people who were popular, even when I was in middle school, and a lot of them don't act like that. It's possible, you know, to be part of the in crowd and not lose your mind and manners over it."

Brynne nods. "That's what I mean, Alli. People who act like that after becoming popular most likely have something to prove, either to themselves or others. Other people are just naturally friendly and draw people to them. They don't try to change for other people. They're just real and balanced."

Brynne twirls a finger through one of her loose curls. It's what she does when she's deep in thought.

"In a world of fake smiles and everyone wanting to be center stage," she continues, "I think it's that authenticity that attracts people—the right kind of people. In the end, when all the smoke clears, we see who's the real deal."

Brynne leans over and pinches my cheek with two fingers. "And everyone shows up to a good person's funeral."

I laugh at the funeral comment, then pat my hands together in mock applause.

"You should think about giving a TedTalk sometime, Brynne. You're good!"

She pushes off the porch post and stands, offering a small bow. "Thank you. Make sure you add that little accolade to your article about me."

Since I've been beating my head against the wall trying to find something more personable to write about Brynne for the article, I just might.

Chapter Nineteen

"Can we talk?"

I stare at him, half in shock, half in fury.

"You're joking, right?"

Chad Barton stands in front of me, partially blocking my exit to freedom and home. I start to plow past him, but he deftly moves back into my path.

"No, Alli, I'm not kidding. It'll only take a second."

Chad shifts slightly to the side to allow a freshman girl to pass, who smiles coyly up at him, before moving back in place. I feel my shoulders trembling under the straps of my backpack but the rest of my body is still as a stone. I'm determined not to show weakness in front of Chad.

I'd rather die first.

A shrill whistle comes from somewhere beyond the door and I will myself not to react. A cluster of rowdy guys pass us and the stench of stale cigarettes lingers in the air behind them, but I ignore that too. My eyes are glued on Chad.

"You can do a lot of damage in a second, Chad. Move. I have nothing to say to you."

Instead of granting my request and moving aside, Chad reaches out and touches my arm, causing me to flinch and jump back. *So much for not reacting.*

I hadn't realized how tightly coiled my nerves are.

"I promise I have nothing up my sleeve. I just need to make something right," he says, his voice pleading. "Please."

Something in his eyes reveals a side of Chad I'd never seen before.

Humbleness? Actual humanity?

Jerking my head to the side, I motion him to move toward a wall of decommissioned lockers. I don't look to see if he follows, I just assume he does. The sound of hollow metal echoes behind me as I fall against an empty locker. I feel safer leaning on something to support my wobbling knees while I give Chad my full attention.

"Make it quick. I'm meeting up with Brynne soon," I say, not sure why he needs to know anything about my plans beyond the school exit doors. Maybe mentioning my plans makes my haste seem more authentic?

Sliding his backpack to the floor, a thoughtful sigh escapes Chad's lips, and I notice his arms grow tense as he crosses them against his chest.

"Listen," he starts, then looks around once before

turning back to me. "I . . . I'm sorry, Alli. Honest." When I start to protest, he throws up a hand. "Please, just let me finish. Like I said, it won't take long."

My chest spasms with short, anxious breaths, and I have to work hard to hide it and maintain the hard, bitter expression on my face. If I don't control my face, I know it will be obvious that my emotions are threatening to take over, and I'll be back at square one with recovering my dignity.

I don't trust my voice, so I just offer a quick nod.

"That whole . . . thing, you know, that happened between us." He thrusts his hand back up, obviously reading that I'm about to lash out. "That was wrong."

His breath comes out in a huff, and he frowns. "Look, I knew it was wrong from the beginning but I . . . I didn't really care at the time. I wanted to go along with the idea because of the, you know, challenge. Plus, the gang was all into the plan, and I didn't want to be on the outs if I didn't go along."

"Oh, yeah, you couldn't have *that*." I snap, then press my lips tight together to keep from saying more.

"I know, lame, right?" He nods sadly. "I was a coward. The thing is, it wasn't even fun anymore after a few days. I wanted out and told Kim that I didn't want to go along with it anymore, that it was a dumb idea. Kim started teasing me, saying that maybe I was starting to really have feelings for you. She got really loud about it, too, and we were around a bunch of the guys and other cheerleaders at football practice. I told her that she was crazy, that there was no way . . ." His eyes widen. "Don't take that wrong, that's not what I mean."

Letting out a breath, he continues, "Anyway, Kim was making a way bigger deal of the whole thing than she should've, and people were listening, so I backed down and just kept up the game. But the more you came to trust me, the worse I started to feel."

I shift my feet, not wanting to hear anymore.

"Why are you telling me all this, Chad? It's over. You had your fun. Why can't you just leave it alone—leave *me* alone?" I say.

Chad looks up at the ceiling, then drops his eyes to mine. "Because, as I got to know you better, the more I hated the game and the angrier I became that I had allowed myself to be pressured into doing that to you. You were—*are*—a really nice girl, Alli, and you . . . well, you didn't deserve that. Under different circumstances, I honestly would've wanted to hang out with you even more than some of the other girls I hang with, you know?"

He studies my face for a moment, which I can only imagine is a canvas of stormy emotions, and quickly moves on.

"What I want to say is, I'm sorry. I can't speak for others, but I'm sorry for putting you through that. I know you won't believe this, but after you saw Kim's message on my phone and ran off like you did, I was sick the rest of the night. I must've picked up my phone to call you a hundred times that night and several days after that, but I couldn't bring myself to do it."

His smile is sad, serious. "You probably wouldn't have answered anyway."

I know he's expecting me to say something. There are a thousand nasty retorts and scathing comments running through my mind, but I can't seem to push any of them down to my lips. Instead, I nod, take an unsteady breath, look past Chad, look at the floor, then back to him.

Eventually, the words come.

"No," I say softly. "I wouldn't have answered."

My gaze drops to the diamond-shaped, multi-colored tiles at my feet. *I've never realized how ugly this floor is,* I think, desperate for a distraction because I'm overwhelmed by this conversation.

Follow this through, Alli.

I push off the locker and force my attention back to Chad. Nodding, I say, "But you could have at least left a message. It would have . . . helped."

But he's already shaking his head. "You wouldn't have believed me, Alli. Not then, maybe not even now."

Chad offers his hand for me to shake. "Forgive me?"

I stare down at his hand but don't touch it. I can't risk it. Can't risk others seeing my hand in his again, setting off sparks that might ignite explosions of gossip. Can't risk falling into an emotional puddle in front of him.

Instead of taking his hand, I wrap both of mine tightly

around the straps of my backpack, maintaining my safe space.

"Okay, Chad," I nod. "Your second's up." I attempt a smile.

It's the best I can do.

"Thanks, Alli," he smiles and backs away.

Chapter Twenty

WE'RE GONNA BE LATE TO SCHOOL. AGAIN.

The second time this week.

"Brynne! Believe it or not, it's okay to go five miles over the speed limit. It's one of those unspoken rules that the cops won't pull you over if you're only going five miles over," I say, knowing my complaining is falling on deaf ears.

Brynne can be impulsive and fun at times, while at other times, she's strait-laced about always following the rules. It drives me crazy sometimes.

That's one thing I miss about Tessa. She always liked to push limits and defy rules, which got us in more trouble than not, but that was way more fun, I think, then realize that comparing Brynne to Tessa is unfair. I push the thought away.

"Relax, Alli," Brynne says. "Mr. Ankor won't even notice that you're missing for the first ten minutes."

She has a point. Mr. Ankor rarely lifts his nose from his

phone or his laptop and only remembers to take attendance about halfway through the period when the front office clerk calls to remind him. Most of the time, there's a stack of worksheets left for us on the desk just inside the door when we come in. He has us well trained to grab a worksheet on our way in and get right to work. As long as we don't bother him, Mr. Ankor doesn't mess with us.

We're also conditioned to know that, when we hear the rustling of him rolling up his daily bag of kale chips, he's about to leave his coveted sanctuary to actually teach us something for the next five to ten minutes. Of course, those are usually only on the days that he's expecting the principal or some other admin staff to come in to observe him.

"Well, aren't you worried about *your* first-period class?" I huff. "You care about breaking the speed limit but not getting to class late?"

To be fair, it's my fault that we're late. I know the status quo for most teenagers is to skip breakfast, but that's not me. I'm already thinking about food the minute my eyes open in the morning. If Mom hasn't made anything for breakfast—which was the case the two times we were late this week because she's been running some early-morning errands for Dad while he's out of town—I have to dig up something to eat for myself.

This morning, I had to wolf down two frozen waffles I had popped into the toaster. I'd managed to spread some syrup on them but had to make do without jelly, which I love. It makes me value all the more the claim that you don't appreciate something until you have to live without it.

Brynne smiles arrogantly. "Need I remind you that I don't have a first period this semester because I only need a few credits to graduate?"

I shake my head and look out the window, watching the traffic creep along in the school zone, as if we weren't going slow enough already.

Yes, I had forgotten Brynne doesn't have a first period. She only goes early with me so she can use the school library to work on her homework for her other classes instead of working on it at home. She claims it's quieter in the library than at her house.

"By the way," she continues, pulling into the student parking lot, where she starts the hunt for an open space. "You never finished telling me what happened with Chad yesterday."

I'm looking around, attempting to help Brynne locate a spot. I had explained most of what happened already, but I think Brynne believes I'm holding something back. I'm not, but she kept asking questions when I called her last night to tell her, as if she thought I had more details than I let on.

"I already told you everything—oh, hey, grab that one," I say, pointing out an open spot between an old blue Honda with rust on the bumper and a cherry-red lifted truck. Brynne turns in, inching herself closer to the nicer truck, assuming the owner will be less likely to carelessly smack their door into her car.

"He apologized," I add. "And I accepted. I'm ready to move on." I start digging through my backpack for my lip balm.

Brynne turns the car off and gives me a pointed look. "And?"

I find it and jerk the cap off. "What do you mean *and?*" I mumble around the tube on my lips.

"Were you wondering if he was, well, hitting on you again or anything?"

The ChapStick hangs midair while I stare at her.

"Hitting on me? Are you serious right now, Brynne?"

She shrugs and unfastens her seatbelt.

"Not hitting on you for a date exactly, but maybe . . ." She flips her hand in the air, palm up. "Just that, possibly, he actually started liking you when he was with you during, you know, that time."

"By *that time* you mean while he was jerking my strings and playing me for a fool?" I snap the tube closed, punctuating the air like a furious conductor. "Like, while he was laughing with his friends in the locker room at my expense, he was secretly nursing a serious crush? Come on, Brynne, be real."

There's no one else in the parking lot, and I know I'm pushing the limit of being late to class to the point that Mr. Ankor may already be taking attendance. That means I'll have to go to the office first for a late pass, which, of course, will be unexcused.

I sigh, and Brynne gives me a look that I interpret to

mean that she thinks I'm about to give in and confess that there really was more to the conversation with Chad than I'm letting on.

"Oh, Alli, don't be so dramatic. I'm just saying that guys have a lot of pride. Even if he did kinda start liking you, he would've kept up his macho camaraderie with his buddies to save face while, you know—"

I jerk the car door open and sling my pack onto my shoulder.

"No, I *don't* know, and I don't *want* to know. Besides— news alert here—I don't care either. That whole ordeal's over, thank goodness, and I'm ready to put it behind me."

Brynne's still sitting in the car when I hop out and lean back in for one last rant.

"And I don't appreciate you calling me dramatic, Brynne. That's just rude."

Just before I slam the door, I hear her call out, "You're welcome for the ride."

I slam the door closed and race to class, hoping that Mr. Ankor hasn't marked me absent yet.

I DON'T MAKE it ten minutes in first period (Mr. Ankor didn't notice me slip in late. Score!) before I text Brynne.

Sorry. I'm a crab this morning. :(

Her reply comes right away.

No breakfast?

She knows me well.
I reply,

If you call frozen waffles bkfst. And no milk
thx to Avery.

I add the emoji with the rolling eyes.

Brynne responds with a green-faced emoji that looks just like I feel: gross. Then, she adds:

It's ok. See u in 2nd?

I text back.

Yep.

I shove my phone under the textbook that I'm using to complete a worksheet on a timeline of the Age of Enlightenment. That is, I'm *supposed* to be filling out this worksheet. But I'm distracted.

I sit and stare down at the empty spaces on the timeline, not one date or event written on the page yet. Mr. Ankor expects our work to be handed in by the end of the period, and, normally, that wouldn't be a problem for me. It's literally as easy as finding dates and plugging them in on the timeline, but I can't even manage to do that.

I'm not still stewing over the spat between Brynne and me. We're cool now. But it's what she said about Chad possibly feeling something genuine while pretending to be all into me to entertain his friends that nags me.

Did Chad really mean it when he said that I'm a nice girl? Was it true that he'd wanted out of the prank but lacked the courage to put a stop to it?

That's part of what rubs me wrong. Even if Chad had wanted to bow out and make things right before they got worse, he didn't. He had the chance, but didn't. I guess Brynne was on track when she said guys will choose pride and saving face over revealing their true feelings.

Mr. Ankor looks up from his laptop and scans the room. I turn a few pages in the textbook and grab my pencil in order to appear busy. Yet, as soon as he turns his attention back to whatever's on his screen, I drop the pencil and lower my chin onto my hand, still staring at the blank worksheet.

I think about how infatuated I had been with Chad Barton. He was good-looking—*very* good-looking—popular, and an athlete. What girl wouldn't be infatuated with him? When I think about it, I have to admit that I was flattered to even be seen with Chad, much less be worthy of his attraction to me.

But I never allowed myself to believe that Chad considered me a serious prospect for a long-term relationship. I accepted that I was probably just another pearl to be added to his string of girl-interests. And I'm ashamed to admit it to myself now, but I was okay with being relegated to the lowly role of being just a temporary distraction for Chad.

To be truthful, I don't know what I thought Chad and I meant to each other. Could I have ever seriously ranked as girlfriend material?

I doubt it. I know better.

But what if I had continued to let myself be dragged along in my fantasy and Chad had taken advantage of my naivety? What if it had gotten to the point that I ended up doing something I'd regret the rest of my life? I think about Tessa and the pain she now carries for the same reason, and my heart aches.

The only thing I know for sure is that Chad made me feel validated as a person, and I'm still not sure why.

Why did I need to feel validated?

As soon as I think it, I already know the answer. I'd felt rejected by Tessa, my pride was at stake, and—this one's the hardest to admit—I had never had a real boyfriend.

Maybe that's why I was so devastated when I discovered that Chad was playing me. The blow was more fatal to my self-esteem than my heart. In hindsight, I see now that I never felt the butterflies that I should've felt when I looked at Chad.

Like the butterflies that come out of nowhere when Anthony's around.

My head shoots up, and I glance around quickly, as if

there might be a mind reader nearby who latched on to my wayward thought. But not one person is looking my way.

Wow, where did that thought even come from? My face floods with heat.

Scooping up my pencil, I jot down the first date I see in the textbook, determined to put Anthony out of my mind, not even sure how thoughts of him and butterflies had crept in there in the first place.

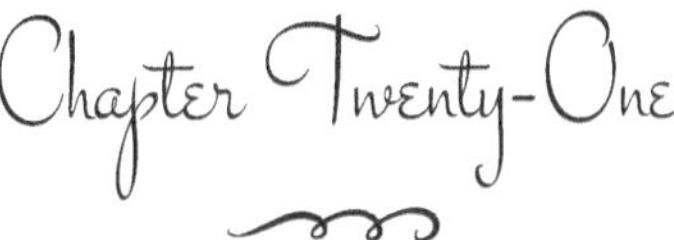

Chapter Twenty-One

"Debbie called this morning," Mom says, setting a steaming plate of waffles down in the center of the table.

I don't bother waiting for anyone else before I reach for the plate. Avery wasn't even awake when I passed her room, and Dad is away on a business trip. Stabbing my fork into two steaming waffles, I drop them onto my plate and reach for the bowl of crushed strawberries.

"Tessa's not doing well."

I look up at Mom over a dripping spoonful of berries and see the worry etched on her forehead.

"What do you mean *not doing well*?" I ask.

Mom pulls out a chair and sinks down into it, pushing a glass carafe of freshly squeezed orange juice closer to me.

"Well, Debbie says she hardly comes out of her room and is failing most of her online classes."

Her sigh drifts over the table and fills the silence in the

room. She picks at the fringe of the linen table runner, straightening each thread until they're lined up in a straight row.

"I guess she hasn't showered for several days. Debbie says the same towel's been hanging in the bathroom—untouched—for days, and Tessa's been in her pajamas since Wednesday."

I cringe. Today is Saturday.

Mom, Avery, and I are going shopping at the mall this afternoon. Fingering the still-damp tip of my braid from my shower, I imagine how gross I'd feel without washing my hair for several days. Hearing that Tessa hasn't showered since Wednesday is unnerving. Especially considering how fastidious Tessa's always been about her looks.

"Wow, that's bad," I say. "Hasn't she been going to see a counselor and all that? I mean, honestly, Mom, Tessa hasn't been *okay* for a long time now, but . . ." Sadness settles over on my shoulders like a heavy blanket. "I thought that she would be, I don't know, getting better by now."

My words sound flat even to my own ears. I can tell by the shadows clouding Mom's normally bright green eyes that she feels the emptiness of the words too.

"It doesn't always work that way, Alli. Not for everyone. A person has to *want* to get better. It takes work, and Tessa is going to have to fight for her life if she's ever going to crawl out of the deep place she's in. A therapist—as well as family and friends—can only help show her the way and support her on her journey to healing, but it's Tessa who will do the work."

She catches my eye across the table. "And God's love can do more to help her heal than any of us can."

I know what she's implying. That I may be the only one who could reach Tessa that way. That our closeness through the years gives me an inroad to Tessa that others might not be able to access. That Tessa would give me an audience that she wouldn't extend to anyone else.

But I haven't had that kind of access to Tessa for months and may never have it again. Especially after she slammed the proverbial door in my face the last time I went to see her.

"I've tried, Mom, I really have. Every time I make the least attempt to have any kind of meaningful conversation with Tessa, she shuts me down." I throw my hands in the air. "I'm sorry. If I honestly thought I could make a differ-ence, I would. But she won't let me in—let anyone in—anymore. We barely get past talking about the weather, as if either of us care about the weather. It's all surface stuff with us. I don't even try to steer the conversation to what happened to her because she gets all hostile and snaps at me."

I hear Avery slamming things around in the bathroom and know she'll be bounding this way any minute now. I shove a huge chunk of waffle in my mouth and reach for the orange juice carafe. I know Mom hates when I talk with my mouth full, so I hope not to do much more talking about the subject.

But halfway through chewing, I finish off with, "And, trust me, Mom, God is the last thing Tessa is interested in discussing."

As predicted, Avery swoops into the kitchen, her purse and a sweater tumbling off one arm.

"You made waffles?! Yessss!"

She dumps her load on the back of the couch, pulls out a chair, and drops herself down with a huff. "I'm starving!" she says.

Mom stands to grab a plate for Avery but doesn't move away from the table for a moment. Instead, she stares down at me with a soft expression on her face.

"I think you're wrong, Alli. Sometimes, when we're most vulnerable and everything feels hopeless is when we are the most receptive to God's voice. And you just might be his voice in her life right now."

Chapter Twenty-Two

Mr. Martin drones on and on about the biological classification of the five kingdoms of living organisms, but I'm barely tuned in.

I've been peering around the collar of Brynne's denim jacket, spying on Shanice, for the past ten minutes.

Her chin rests in the palm of her hand as she stares at Mr. Martin with a glazed expression. I doubt she's listening any more than I am. Not that glazing over when Mr. Martin lectures is out of the ordinary. His lectures can be pretty boring.

No one gives a hoot about classifying organisms—except maybe Zach, who sits across from me, studiously scribbling notes and has half a page filled out already.

But it's Shanice spacing out in her own world instead of participating in the obvious goofing off by the other kids around her that catches my attention. I've never seen

Shanice miss an opportunity to be the center of attention of anything or at least not join in the mischief other people stir up.

"Alli? Yes, or no?"

At the sound of my name, my head jerks toward the front of the room, where Mr. Martin is poised with a marker in his hand, ready to fill in a square on a chart he's drawn on the board. He must notice the panic on my face and that I have no clue what he's asking me about because he generously repeats the question.

"Is a nuclear membrane present in a protist cell?"

I still have no clue. Looking at Brynne is no help either. She just shrugs.

Mr. Martin turns to Zach.

"Zach?"

Zach doesn't even look up from his paper when he answers. "Yeah, they have nuclear membranes around their DNA."

"Yes," Mr. Martin says.

He stares right at me as he addresses the class. "You might want to copy this chart down in your notebook. There's a quiz on this next topic next Tuesday."

I pull my notebook closer and start copying the board. About halfway through the chart, I glance over at Shanice and see that she's hunched over a piece of paper, also copying the chart and oblivious to the chatter at her table.

"What are you staring at?" Brynne whispers. I glance

back to the board and fill in another box in my chart. "Nothing."

When I finish writing, I look up. Brynne is still staring at me. One eyebrow lifts, and she looks over her shoulder toward Shanice, then back to me.

"Right. Did you two have another awkward moment in the bathroom again?"

Zach acts like he isn't listening, but he's been erasing the same blank spot on his paper for way too long. I give my head a little shake to warn Brynne not to ask any more questions.

"Later," I mouth.

When Zach slips off his chair and walks over to ask Mr. Martin something and Brynne is busy sliding her notebook into her satchel, I steal another glance at Shanice.

She's staring out the window, chewing on the end of her pencil. Without warning, she turns to look my way, and I drop my eyes and start flipping through the pages in my notebook like I'm searching for something.

Busted.

I finish up my notes and pull out my school laptop to check my grades and see if I'm missing any assignments, just to have something to do.

I don't dare look over at Shanice again the rest of the period.

Chapter Twenty-Three

After several rings, her voicemail finally picks up. I wasn't ready for it and fumble through a lame message.

"Hey, it's Alli. Just checking on you. Hope everything's okay," I say, before quickly ending the call.

I feel like I should've said more, but I hate leaving recorded messages. There's something about how weird my voice sounds played back on voicemail.

Well, I guess I've done my part. The ball's in her court now.

Before I set the phone down, it rings. A smiling image of Tessa fills the screen, a photo I'd taken of her last summer when she came with me and my family to the Grand Canyon. I'm terrified of heights, so I was the only one of us who hadn't posed daringly close to the canyon edge, choosing instead to stand so far back that I only had a limited view of the top of the rim. I was fine with that. But Tessa had a great time, the proof in the photo being her jubilant smile as she posed in front of the South Rim.

I used to have a special ringtone for Tessa that played the song "You've Got a Friend in Me." I changed her ringtone not too long ago to a generic one since, you know, we aren't best friends anymore and only best friends get the privilege of a special ringtone.

I tap the answer button and raise the phone to my ear.

"Hey, Tessa, that was fast."

My voice sounds friendly and more excited than it should, especially after how my last visit with Tessa ended. But I always sound excited when I'm nervous.

"Yeah," she answers. "I saw it was you calling. I'm ignoring most of my calls."

Part of me is flattered that I passed Tessa's "ignoring most calls" test and that she's willing to talk to me, while the other part of me is curious about *why* she's avoiding talking to other people.

"Ah, got it. Well, I'm glad you called back. I know . . ." I hesitate, trying to decide whether to bring it up or pretend it never happened. "Um, I know things didn't end too well the last time we talked."

Even though I *did all the talking while she was zoning out*, I think. But there's no point in bringing that up.

"Anyhow, I'm sorry, Tessa. I really have missed talking to you and thought we could, you know, catch up."

Naturally, I don't plan to mention that her mom called my mom because she was worried about Tessa. I don't tell

Tessa that everyone thinks I have this great connection with her and can pull her out of her funk when, in reality, I have little to no connection with Tessa these days.

And, naturally, Tessa would already know that I've tried a hundred times to draw her out with no success. But, here I am, calling her and making another go at it.

Dependable old Alli, being the Good Samaritan once again is what I imagine is going through Tessa's head right now.

"It's all good. Honest. I'm . . . I'm glad you called," Tessa says.

You are? I say, then realize that I didn't actually voice it out loud and try again. "You are?" The shock in my voice is unmistakable.

"Yeah, I am. I thought about calling you a few times."

And you didn't because . . . ?

"Oh," I mumble instead.

"So what have you been up to?" she asks.

"Nothing much. You?"

Dumb question, Alli. You know she's been holed up in her room.

"Same here," she says.

A long silence hangs in the air before she speaks again.

"So, uh, are you busy tonight?" she asks. "I mean, do you want to come over?"

Her tone is flat and lacks the enthusiasm one would expect from an invitation to hang out, but her request sounds sincere. I quickly consider what I have going on tonight. The only thing I come up with is that it's my night to wash dishes.

"Sure," I say. "Maybe around 7ish?" I figure dinner and dishes should be wrapped up by then.

"Yeah, that sounds good," she says.

It feels like the conversation should end here. We've made our plans and our little chat can obviously be picked up later when we're face-to-face, but I hesitate because it doesn't feel right to end the call yet.

"So," I say. "Are you doing okay?"

Again, I feel dumb and want to kick myself as soon as I say it because I already know the answer, courtesy of Tessa's mom. But Tessa doesn't know about Debbie's call, and I have to play it off.

"I mean, is everything going—"

"—I'm okay, Alli," she cuts in. "Thanks for asking though."

Of course, now we both know she's lying, but we're both content to end the call with the lie.

"Oh, that's great," I say. "I'll see you tonight then."

I FIND her on the back porch, reading a book.

She's wearing dingy grey sweatpants that are so wrinkled that I'm sure she either slept in them or just pulled them out of the laundry basket right before I arrived. An oversized sweatshirt that I've seen her dad wear on a few occasions hangs on her like a deflated parachute.

Her feet are bare, one of them tucked under her hip as

she curls into the faded cotton cover of a porch chair. Her head is down, and I can't see her face under the waterfall of stringy auburn hair that hangs in front of it. It takes me a second to get over the shock of her unkempt appearance before I recover.

"Whatcha reading?"

Tessa flinches and jerks her head up. I hadn't meant to scare her. She must've really been into her book not to hear the obvious screeching of the rusty screen door when I pushed through it. Her eyes are wide, but she bounces back quickly and snaps the book shut, dropping it down on the table.

I glance at the cover and see the title: *Girl in Pieces*.

"Nothing. Just a book Shanice dropped off. I'm not that into it."

At the sound of Shanice's name, I look up sharply as I lower myself into a chair across from Tessa.

"Shanice came to see you?" I blurt out before I can pull back the irritation in my voice. A thousand warning bells clang in my skull, wondering what in the world Shanice wants with Tessa and how more trauma is the last thing Tessa needs in her life right now.

But the question doesn't seem to faze Tessa at all as she hitches one shoulder and says, "She comes by once in a while." Then, as if to appease the tension I know she's sensing in me, she adds, "She doesn't stay long."

I still can't seem to reign in my indignation.

"Yeah, but why does she even come by? I mean, after everything—"

"—She had nothing to do with what happened that night, Alli."

Tessa fixes her gaze on me. It's the most direct connection we've made in a long time.

I want to lash out. To tell her that Shanice was the one that dragged her into the whole party scene in the first place and had played a key role in influencing Tessa to become the person that was the distinct opposite of the person who I'd known and adored. That it was Shanice's slimy pit of losers who led Tessa to make dumb choices that will forever haunt her.

But I can't say all that—I have no right to say it—because I've already thought about it all these months and realize that no one can make you do what you don't want to do. Tessa did all that to herself. Shanice just provided the opportunities.

I'm the first to break away and drop my eyes to the ground. "I guess," I say.

"Look, I know you didn't like Shanice—"

"—Still don't," I mumble, still not looking at her.

"Fine," she sighs. "That you *don't* like Shanice, and I get it. She was awful to you, and there were times I didn't like her either."

I meet her eyes. "Then why were you friends with her? Why are you *still* friends with her? Why did you stand by and watch her treat me like that and still hang around her?

What did she and Kim do to make you turn against me like you did?"

I don't know how we got here so fast. I really don't. My plan was to come here to comfort and be there for Tessa. I haven't been here for five minutes, and we're already slashing open some painful wounds.

Tessa doesn't break her focus on me, and it's then that I understand that this is something more, something profound. This is an answer to prayer.

Tessa's talking. *Really* talking.

I can feel her sigh press into me from across the table, and I know this is hard for her. But she seems to rally, and I can't help but be proud of the transformation she has made since we were together last.

"I . . . I don't know, Alli. I just . . . don't know what happened, you know, to me—to us. Why did I choose to do a lot of things that I did? I didn't have an ounce of feelings for that guy . . ."

Her voice trails off, and, even though the final rays of sunlight are fading, and dusk is encroaching on the last of our light, the tear on Tessa's cheek is unmistakable. My own eyes sting, and it takes me a moment before I fully grasp what she's really saying.

The life that she threw away. The baby.

"Oh, Tessa."

I want to rush over and throw my arms around her— and I'd have already done that if I wasn't so insecure about how Tessa would receive it.

I want to tell her that I'm sorry that she's bleeding from so many wounds that, just when she gets one bound up, another one breaks open. I've learned never to tell someone that you know what they're going through when you clearly don't have the slightest clue.

I'm ashamed that the closest comparison I can come up with is that some guy maliciously broke my heart in front of everyone. Yet, this pales against Tessa's crippling regrets, loss of innocence, and deep scars that she will bear for a lifetime.

But I can still listen. And learn.

Chapter Twenty-Four

SHE DOESN'T BOTHER TO BRUSH AWAY THE MOISTURE THAT puddles on her chin. Tessa's either so lost in her thoughts that she doesn't notice them, or she is finally acknowledging her feelings.

Maybe both.

Another tear runs down her cheek. Then another, until they meet and blend into twin rivers, overflowing the puddle on her chin and flowing down her neck. My own cheeks are wet with tears. I don't bother to wipe them away either.

"My mom has been taking me to see a therapist once a week to *talk about my feelings*," Tessa says, her hands forming air quotes along with her words. "And when the therapist is done hammering me with questions that I don't want to answer, my mom picks it up from there on the way home."

She releases a shaky breath and wipes her runny nose

with a sleeve. The porch light flickers on with the waning sunlight, casting a soft glow down on us that makes Tessa's damp skin look like warped glass.

"They all want me to talk about what happened in New Mexico." She exhales and casts a dark look my way.

"Mom, Dad, the therapist, everyone at school, the media, the stupid mailman—*everyone*! They all want every single one of the dirty details. For me to spill the whole story so they actually have something to document and analyze—to talk about—instead of just the blank stares and silence they usually get from me. Well, I'm not giving them what they want. Does anyone stop to think about what I want, or what I *don't* want? Can't I just try to overcome all the horror and revulsion without having to bleed out in front of everyone?"

I notice the tremble of her delicate shoulders as she looks away, off into some far-off distance, her expression longing and mournful, as if she would sprout wings and take flight if she had the ability to.

She turns back to me with haunted eyes.

"Why? Why do they *need* to know? Are they wanting a good story to make a documentary or something out of it? Do they need a tragic case study to support their campaign for 'This could happen to your daughter if . . . ?'" Again, she emphasizes with air quotes.

She jerks her body around to fully face me, leaning so hard against the table that I have to press into it to keep it from toppling onto my lap.

"They don't get it. I. Don't. Want. To. Talk. About. It. I would *love* to forget about it—like that's possible—and sleep one night without the nightmares," she says with an anguished cry that sounds as if her heart is being torn from her chest.

In a way, I think it is.

"I just want to forget about what those . . . those . . . guys did to me—*with* me—for a little while because—" I can see Tessa's struggling to go on, gulping down the hysteria rising in her voice. "And that's not the only plague that torments my dreams at night. There's so much more that haunts me, so many other demons crawling on my back."

She's nearly panting, her breaths hard and fast, looking between me and the tilted edge of the table. Then, the dam breaks, and Tessa throws her face into her hands and lets the flood take her away.

I barely make out her next words.

"At least I was, you know, drugged up. I . . . didn't really know what was happening half of the time. Gosh," she sobs, "I didn't *choose* . . . didn't *mean*, to end up there. No one believes me. It just happened before I even knew what was going on."

Her voice is tremulous and low, and I have to strain my body forward to catch her next words.

"But . . . but, I *knew* . . . I was wide awake, Alli . . . I *knew* what I was doing when . . ."

Her words drown under an avalanche of emotion that

sweeps her under. I sit quietly for a moment and let her cry. Not because I don't want to reach out or find a way to comfort her but because I don't know *how*, or where, to even start.

She sobs for a minute or two, and I begin to wonder if she even remembers that I'm still here—if it even matters whether I'm here or not.

Easing the table back on all four legs, slowly and carefully so I don't disturb her, I'm just now feeling the chill against my own cheeks as damp tears cover them.

Table back in place, I settle like a statue, still unwilling to disrupt the flow of Tessa's release. I don't move, don't try to say anything, as if I could think of anything to say right now anyway.

This is her private moment of cleansing and what I hope is the first step in healing, and I refuse to mess it up.

It's not until she blows her nose that I look up from the twisting of my fingers in my lap. She's looking at me, and I can tell she's expecting a response. It's probably just now hitting her that I haven't said a word, and Tessa knows me better than that.

Well, at least she *used* to know how I'd normally have tried to offer advice or jump up to hug her and tell her everything's gonna be okay.

Maybe she doesn't realize that she's not the only one who has changed over these months. It's not that I've become callous and uncaring, or that I'm being overcautious in opening up to her after all we've been through—which I probably am, actually.

No, I think it's that I've learned to use wisdom and to be a better listener. Instead of an instant reaction, I see the worthiness of a delayed response, just to make sure I'm on the right track before jumping ahead and throwing my emotions out there before thinking about things first.

Which is a good thing because, had I jumped in to try and rescue and comfort Tessa as soon as the dam broke, she may have never had the chance to get things off her chest.

She might not have unloaded what bothered her more than what we had all assumed. The horror that would have most obviously been the source of anguish for most of us wasn't what was dragging Tessa under.

I took care of it, she told me all those months ago.

The pregnancy. The *baby*.

It made sense now. She'd been a victim—against her will—to a heinous crime and subjected to horrible physical abuse. But flushing her body of the evidence of a pregnancy was a result of her own free will.

I wonder at the depth of her pain because Tessa doesn't share my faith and doesn't hold herself to the same standards that I do as a Christian. So why would it matter so much to her?

"I'm so sorry, Tessa," I say. "I didn't . . . know how much that bothered you. I mean—"

"—You think I don't feel regret or have any moral standards or *feelings* just because I'm not a Christian?" she cuts in.

"I may not feel like, you know, living how you live," she waves a hand from my head to my feet, obviously taking in my long hair and modest skirt, "but that doesn't mean I don't believe in God or care about a human life, Alli."

Her brows furrow and she shakes her head.

"It's *because* you're a Christian that I couldn't talk to you about it. I wanted to." She sniffed. "I wanted to so badly. I can't tell you how many times I stared at your number on my phone and wanted to hit the button to call, but . . . didn't."

"Why didn't you?" I whisper. "Why didn't you think you could call me? I've never judged you, Tessa. You know that."

Her gaze is direct and clear, in spite of the red, glassy eyes.

"You don't have to say anything to make me feel judged, Alli. I know what you stand for and that you wouldn't have been able to help yourself from feeling that I was a horrible person for what I chose to do. It's just woven into your makeup—what you've always believed. How could I have expected you to feel differently? Would you have understood and thought it was the right decision considering the situation?"

One finger wags in the air as she shakes her head.

"Don't answer that. I already know. I didn't have to call you or even need to hear your voice to know that you were already disappointed in me. I saw it written all over your face that day, the day I told you I'd done it. Your look alone voiced loud and clear what you never said but wanted to."

She releases a long breath. "So I wasn't about to call you and go through another guilt session."

I'm stunned. Genuinely stunned. Am I really that easy to read? Judging by Tessa's observation, apparently I am.

I try to imagine what my expression must have looked like on the day she told me that she'd "taken care of it," meaning that she'd already had the abortion and there was nothing more to say. She was subtly letting me know that she didn't need my input on the matter and that she wanted me to never bring it up again.

Why had she even told me? I wonder. *Was it just to shut me up so I wouldn't keep questioning her about it?*

Considering it now, it frustrates me.

What did she expect me to feel? Of course, I was shocked. I hadn't even had time to process what she told me before she shut me down and walked away. Did Tessa honestly believe that the only thing I had felt was judgment and didn't care at all about what it must have done to her to go through that?

I am—*was*—her best friend.

Regardless of the silence and distance between us at the time, we had shared a childhood and a lifetime's worth of intimacy and memories together.

Not only had Tessa faced the devastation of her parents' divorce without me, but she'd also had to come to terms with an unexpected pregnancy, and, knowing Tessa as I do, a panicked decision to end it—alone.

I doubt any of her posh new friends held her hand and wiped her tears through it all.

Did any of them even go with her to the clinic or wherever she'd gone to have the procedure? Was she alone for that too?

No, being the "great" friends that they were, they probably laughed at her for being so stupid as to get pregnant in the first place. The only kindness they might have shown was to take up a collection to pay for the procedure.

That's not what a *real* friend would have done—not what *I* would have done.

What was it about me that made Tessa feel like she couldn't reach out to me?

"Tessa, I'm sorry. I truly am. I never . . . never meant to come across like that. Yes, I was shocked. I mean, who wouldn't be? But I didn't judge you or think less of you."

I run my palms across my eyes and let out a long, shaky breath.

"Okay, that's not completely honest. I *was* disappointed but I . . . I know you felt like you didn't have a choice. I just feel so bad that you had to, you know, face that alone. We've done some stupid things together that I'm not proud of, so I had no right to . . . to judge you. I just wish we could have talked first, that I could have been there for you."

I feel the corners of my mouth sag as the weight of it all floods over me.

"You never told your mom and dad, did you?"

She shakes her head but doesn't look away. "No. I couldn't. My mom was already so depressed over the divorce. There was no way—"

"—I understand, Tessa. I know you have your reasons. That's not why I'm asking." I take a moment to stop myself from veering off into a lecture she doesn't want or need.

"It's just that you shouldn't have faced that alone. There are people who care about you—"

"—Come on, Alli."

I jump at the intensity of her interruption, and the fire in her eyes burns through me like she'd thrown hot coals in my face.

"You know what finding out I was pregnant would have done to our family, on top of everything else. Aaron was already giving Mom and Dad a hard time, sneaking out and causing problems at school. Mom blamed herself—like it was *her* fault that Dad left and that Aaron couldn't handle it. Can you *imagine* if she'd found out her daughter was pregnant on top of it all? Think about it, Alli. I might as well have thrown lighter fluid on her and watched her burn because that's what it would have done to her—killed her."

I hadn't realized how bad things must have been at home for Tessa or her mom. I hadn't even considered what her brother, Aaron, was feeling through all of it either.

I'd run out of words, which is fine because I'm fairly sure Tessa had too.

I walk over and pull her out of her chair and throw my

arms around her. We cling to each other like that for a while, crying and slobbering all over each other.

It's a best friend moment.

And which one of us needs this moment more doesn't matter.

Chapter Twenty-Five

SHE'S SITTING ON A BENCH IN FRONT OF THE SCHOOL WHEN I notice her.

I'm standing under a tree near the street, waiting for my mom to pick me up to go shopping for something to wear for graduation photos.

Brynne had planned to tag along—overachiever that she is, she'd had her photos done two weeks ago—but forgot she had a dentist appointment and left school early to go. She told me I had to send her pics of potential outfits so she could "approve" them first so I didn't look like a clown in photos I'd have to look at for the rest of my life.

I told her to jump off a bridge and that I had already been eyeing a striking neon-green jogging outfit that fit perfectly in my price range. She got a good laugh out of that, but I caught the slight look of panic in her expression that I might really do it.

Shanice is alone on the bench, scrolling through her cell phone. A quick look around tells me that none of her cheer team cronies or friends are anywhere close by.

Is she meeting them here? I wonder.

I doubt it because I never see them when I walk home this way when I either don't catch a ride with Brynne or Dad needs to borrow his old car from me for something. It's rare to spot any of the popular kids on the side of the building where you either board a school bus, get picked up, or are walking home. A few have bikes and skateboards they park next to the side gate.

But the cool, popular kids? Either they have their own set of wheels or lots of friends who do. Only losers leave from the front doors of the school.

Which is why I'm surprised to see Shanice out here. Alone.

My phone chirps, and I glance down at the screen to see a text from Mom saying that she's running a few minutes late. I tap out a quick message.

K. See u soon

Slipping my phone back into my skirt pocket, I look around. The crowd leaving the school thins, and the sound of traffic and birds descending on discarded food remnants replace the turbulence of students that had been here only moments before.

All the buses are gone, leaving a few stragglers waiting for rides or just hanging around for who knows why.

My curiosity is pulled back to Shanice, who's still engrossed in something on her phone screen. I really don't care to sit on the steps with all the discarded chip bags, fresh wads of gum, and crumpled papers, and just looking at the grass gives me hives. Besides, I'm not into frolicking with bugs and damp soil.

Shanice is sitting alone on the only bench out here, and there's plenty of room for two. I start walking.

"Hey, is anyone sitting here?" I ask, knowing full well that no one is but not wanting her to know I've been watching her for five minutes and haven't seen a soul come anywhere near her. Phone still in hand, she looks my way. I see the recognition in her eyes. It's a pleasant surprise that, for once, she doesn't look disgusted or offended by the sight of me.

"No, you're good," she says and tugs her backpack closer to make space for me even though there's plenty of room for both of us already.

"Thanks."

I tug my backpack off and set it on the ground at my feet before lowering myself to the bench as close to the opposite edge from her as possible.

Not for my comfort, but for hers.

I watch as a young couple strolls past, heads together, whispering and giggling as if they existed in a world of their own, before they disappear down the street. There's a lull in traffic, and even the birds have gone silent, probably bloated and drowsy from their feast of greasy chips and sandwich crusts.

I find myself hoping that my mom will be later than whomever Shanice is waiting for because I'm helplessly curious about why she's sitting out here. I know the feeling isn't mutual because she probably expects me—someone from the lower class—to be waiting in front of the school for a ride.

Not expecting it, I flinch when she speaks.

"Are you waiting for someone?"

I'm a little surprised she would ask since I would think that's obvious, but I answer smoothly, "Yeah, my mom. We're going shopping for something to wear for graduation pics."

I hesitate before asking, "You?"

She doesn't answer for moment, and I turn away, figuring she either didn't hear me or is ignoring the question. I'm also still processing that I'm actually sitting on a bench and having a civil conversation with Shanice, elite cheerleader and my number one nemesis for most of this school year.

"No," she finally replies in a breathy whisper. "I'm waiting for them to . . . leave."

I study her face as she glances over her shoulder at the school before turning back and fixing her eyes on something across the street. Her face is a stone, devoid of emotion, so I don't know how to respond.

Who's she hiding from and why?

I don't have the gall to ask and figure that, if I'm quiet long enough, she might continue talking on her own. She does.

"I hate them all."

I blink. I wasn't expecting anything like that, and I almost regret my intrusion by coming over here. If she's mad at her friends and spews all her venom on me, only to kiss and make up with them later, that means she'll lash out at me even more because I saw her in a weak moment. I've had all the negative attention I can handle for this year.

"Oh, sorry," I say.

"I don't expect you to care. I know you hate me anyway, and I guess I don't blame you." She swivels her gaze my way. "You probably think I deserve every bit of it and more."

She lost me there. I have an idea, but honestly don't know exactly what she's talking about. Sure, I don't like her, have even hated her at times, but whatever she's referring to that she thinks I believe she deserves doesn't register.

"Shanice, I don't hate you. Well, at this moment anyway. There were times I did, but, well, it doesn't matter. Anyhow, I don't think you deserve—I don't know—I mean." I let out a huff of breath. "I don't even know what happened or what you're talking about."

One eyebrow raises. "You don't?"

She snorts and turns her head away. "You must be

living under a rock if you don't know. I thought everyone knew."

I should be hurt by the living-under-a-rock comment, but, surprisingly, I'm not. Girls like Shanice just assume that the whole world is interested in their comings and goings and spend their days discussing them as if the rest of us—the unpopular ones—are soaking up their lives like an addiction to a reality show.

But we aren't. At least I'm not, and neither is anyone I'm around at school. I guess that means that me and my friends aren't included in the "everyone" population.

"No, I haven't heard anything about you, and I don't need to. Whatever it is, I'm sure it will blow over."

I lean my head forward, peeking to see if my mom's car is coming down the road yet, ready to make a hasty exit from this conversation and whatever drama Shanice is hinting at. She must be pretty desperate if she is telling *me*, of all people, her troubles.

A lone car makes its way around the corner and pulls up in front of where we're sitting. I stand and scoop up my backpack.

"Well, hey, I hope everything works out," I say as I shoulder my pack.

"Thanks," she mumbles. "I guess I have an idea of how you felt after, you know, the whole thing with Chad." Her voice catches with emotion.

I stop and turn back around to face her.

She's looking up at me with a sad smile and glistening

eyes. I feel the tug on my heart because there's a vulnerability in her eyes that I don't feel right walking away from. I know my mom wouldn't mind waiting, but, when I think about how Shanice never cared when I was in a vulnerable place, I feel my compassion extinguish as quickly as it came.

"No, Shanice, I don't think so. You don't know me that well, so you have no idea how I felt after Chad destroyed me in front of everyone."

I spin on my heel and make my way to the waiting car.

Chapter Twenty-Six

"Oh, *that*." Brynne shrugs. "I thought everyone knew."

I throw my hands up. "You know *what*? Am I the only one of *everyone* who doesn't know?"

We're standing in line at Starbucks, and there are two people in front of Brynne. My outburst prompts stares from the people in line and those waiting for orders at a nearby counter. I'm almost sure a few even move closer to eavesdrop on our conversation.

And why not? I'm sure they all want to know what *everyone* knows that, apparently, *I* don't know.

Brynne ignores my tantrum.

"Yeah, Shanice was at some party recently and ended up sneaking off with some guy named Tyler—remember the basketball player with the red hair at pep rally last Friday, the one with the nose piercing?"

I shake my head. "No clue. Go on."

"Anyhow, Shanice goes off with him, and no one saw them the rest of the night, if you know what I mean. Chad and some of the other guys were teasing her about it in front of Kim, and Kim was livid. They had an all-out cat fight—"

"Wait!" I say, one hand waving in front of her face. "I'm lost. Why would Kim care what Tyler and Shanice were doing?"

Brynne shakes her head. "Tyler is Kim's boyfriend, of course."

"Oh, yes, *of course*," I mimic. "I should have known that, riiiight."

"Oh, stop rolling your eyes at me. He and Kim have been an item for weeks," Brynne tries to explain and huffs. "Are you on another planet or something?"

She points to the sky and forms her hands around an imaginary planet.

"Really, Alli? How can you miss them? The two of them are always together."

I shrug. "I don't pay any attention to Kim or that crowd, Brynne. You know that. When's the last time you saw me anywhere near them?"

"They parade around the whole campus, Alli. You can't miss them," Brynne says.

I drop it.

"Anyhow," I say. "Back to Shanice. I'm guessing that's what she was referring to when she claims that they all hate her. It also explains why she's suddenly become a loner." I shrug. "Well, what did she expect if she was messing around with another girl's boyfriend—*Kim's* of all people? She should've known she was asking for trouble, and now she's got it. I don't feel sorry for her one bit."

Brynne stares at me, her eyes narrowing. "Wow, nice attitude, Alli."

She's temporarily distracted when the line shifts as the first person finishes and steps away. Brynne takes a step forward, then whips back around to face me. She doesn't look away as one hand digs around in her purse for her wallet.

"What?" I shrug again. "What do you want me to say?"

Her other hand slides to her hip. "You said she was an emotional mess when you saw her in the bathroom and on that bench after school and that everyone—"

"Argh, don't say *everyone* again." I groan.

"Fine, *almost* everyone at school is labeling her as a—well, I won't repeat what they're calling her—and her reputation is ruined. She doesn't have a friend left on campus, Alli. Think about that for a minute. How can you be so cold?"

My cheeks grow warm.

"Didn't she think about all that before she went off with this guy, Tyler, or whatever his name is? I mean, yeah, it's sad. She probably won't live it down for the rest of the school year now, and, based off Tessa's experience, she's way better off without them. Maybe this will help her in the end. After graduation, she doesn't have to ever see any of them again. Am I right?"

Brynne points her wallet at me like she's about to smack me on the nose with it. I know we still have an audience, but I ignore the onlookers as Brynne glares at me between wallet jabs.

"Yeah, Alli, that all worked out really well for Tessa now, didn't it?" Brynne says. "Maybe, and that's a *maybe*, she'll never have to face them again, but that doesn't mean she's not hurting. You can't always run away and hide from people. It's not that simple."

It's Brynne's turn in line. After giving the barista her order, she turns back to me, her expression neutral, as if she's determined that I'm a hopeless case.

"I'm gonna grab that table in the corner. Can you get our drinks when they're ready?" she says and hurries off.

When the drinks and my toasted bagel are ready, I scoop them up and make my way to the table, where Brynne is tapping away on her laptop. Setting everything on the table, I slide onto a chair.

"It's not the same," I continue, spreading a thick layer of cream cheese on my bagel. The bagel is still steaming, and my fingers dance as I try to keep my grip on it.

Brynne peeks at me over the top of her laptop. "What's not the same?"

"Tessa. She went through something way more horri-fying than Shanice is facing and you know it."

Brynne snaps the lid down on her laptop.

"I meant before the . . . *that* happened. You could see it written all over Tessa's face, Alli. She never really fit in. She wasn't happy. All you had to do was look at her to know Tessa was hurting. Maybe other people missed it, but I could tell she was like a puppy lost in the woods. On top of that, most people didn't even know about her family situation or how she had lost her best friend."

"*Lost* her best friend?" I snap. "More like *dumped* her best friend. I don't think that was much of a traumatic experience for her, Brynne. For sure, her parents' divorce and all, but not losing out on having me as a friend. I'd think that was obvious."

Brynne doesn't answer, and I don't continue.

We sip our drinks and allow our tempers to cool while we watch a toddler at the next table scoop out spoonfuls of whipped cream from a paper cup. I guess dogs aren't the only ones eligible to get a Puppuccino when they come to Starbucks.

The small boy, whom I guess to be around three years old, smiles triumphantly over at us with a creamy mustache, making both Brynne and I break out in giggles. We wave at him and give him flirty smiles. With a captive audience, he becomes more animated and ends up flicking the woman next to him, who I assume is his mom, with a dollop of whipped cream. She tugs him back down in his seat and gives him a stern scolding.

I turn back to Brynne.

"Fine. You're right," I say. "I could be a little less judgmental, but you can't blame me for being cautious."

"Less judgmental?" She winces as she swallows a mouthful of hot coffee. "That's it?"

"Okay, then, I'll invite her over to your house the next time I come over. We can have a slumber party and make popcorn. Sound good?"

I lift my cup in a toast.

Brynne picks up her napkin and throws it at me.

"You're hopeless, Alli."

Chapter Twenty-Seven

Mrs. Monroe is my favorite teacher.

Now, anyway. She didn't used to be. At one time in my mind, she had been a stereotypical grandma and should-have-retired-years-ago teacher.

She wears her silver-gray hair piled up in a messy bun on top of her head. Not the cute, carefree messy bun that busy young moms and trendy women working out at the gym have. Mrs. Monroe's bun is more like a bird's nest thrown together by a stressed-out momma bird needing a place to drop her eggs—only to have a windstorm sweep in to make matters worse.

When she's angry, Mrs. Monroe's bird's nest nods with the bounce of her head while she rains fire and brimstone down on an unruly class. Not only does it bob, but it also sways sideways when she delivers a heartfelt extolment about a piece from a written work that she's passionate about.

Like when she reads a passage from Frederick Douglass or Shakespeare's *Othello* from the 1600s, where most of us have no clue what she's talking about because—let's be honest—no one talks like they did in the 1600s anymore.

When Mrs. Monroe's bun starts its rotation, it requires extreme self-discipline not to burst out laughing and subject the whole class to lunch detention.

One mistake you never want to make is to show up late to her class, especially if she's in a bad mood. She takes it as a personal insult, and it doesn't matter if you've been throwing up in the hallway or you've been hit by a bus on the way to school.

If you're late, you are in for it.

Anyhow, Mrs. Monroe and I get along great now, but it wasn't always that way.

For instance, I was the unlucky recipient of one of Mrs. Monroe's exceptional tirades when I dared to show up late to class one day. Unlucky for her, I was *also* in a mood that day and gave it right back to her.

Bad move.

But surprisingly, everything ended well when we took it to the hallway and cooled off enough to discuss things civilly—and honestly. She even apologized and made me feel like she really cared about why I'd behaved so out of character. I needed her compassion in that moment, and, well, I've liked Mrs. Monroe ever since.

Still, when she calls my name, my heart slides down to my stomach.

"Alli, can you come here, please?"

She says it pleasantly, but I still get the whispered "Oh, you're in for it now" comments on my way to her desk, where she's sitting and squinting up at something on her desktop screen. I approach and stand quietly, waiting for her to notice me.

"Please, have a seat."

She gestures toward the extra chair next to the desk.

"I want to show you something."

She's talking quietly, so as not to disturb the rest of the class as they work on an essay that's due next week. The one I haven't even started yet. But she doesn't know that.

Mrs. Monroe uses both hands to turn her computer screen my way, and I peer over at it. There's a glare from the overhead lights, so I can't really see what's on display.

"Um, I don't know—" I start to say, but she chimes in with, "—It's a short story contest. I think you should submit a piece."

I sit back and eye her. "Short story contest?" I ask.

"Yes, yes. I've seen some inspiring work from you this semester, and I believe you should give it a shot."

Her smile is warm and energetic, like she's just invited me over to her house for a cup of tea. I can see the contest idea appeals to her, and I want to tell her that maybe *she* should be the one submitting a story instead of me.

But I smile back—less energetically than she does, of course—and tilt my chin.

"I'm not sure, Mrs. Monroe. I've never written anything I'd even think about submitting for a contest. I'm not good at making up stories. I do better with factual stuff and opinion pieces, like the stuff I write for the *Morrison Tribute*."

"Nonsense," she scowls. "You won't be writing opinion pieces for the school newspaper forever."

She waves a hand dismissively in the air. Her voice squeaks just above a whisper, prompting a few students in the front row to glance up. It's not like they haven't already been straining to overhear our conversation anyway. I'm sure everyone's—*Oops, not everyone. Why is that word a burr in my side lately?*—no, I'm sure *most* in the class are curious about the special attention I'm getting by being called to the teacher's desk and being privy to some exciting news on her computer screen.

I'm hoping they don't think Mrs. Monroe is so ecstatic over my stellar classwork that she just couldn't wait to share my excellent grade with me (which has been unheard of in my high school career). That would be awful. I'd be labeled a teacher's pet for the rest of the year and would never hear the end of it.

Without waiting for my reply, she hits a button on her keyboard, and a machine whirs to life behind her. With one swift motion, she plucks the paper from the printer and presents it to me like a coveted prize. I take it in my fingers and pull it against my chest, hoping I can make it back to my desk without anyone noticing, which about as likely as a hundred-dollar bill falling from the sky.

Still clutching the page to my body, I nod and stand, hoping she's done because I feel more sets of curious eyes looking our way.

"Thanks," I mumble. "I'll look this over and get back with you."

"The deadline is in three weeks."

Mrs. Monroe winks and raises from her desk as I turn to leave.

She walks around her desk and stands in front of a boy with dyed blue hair and a shower of freckles on his cheeks. I almost believe she chose him on purpose because he was the most interested in our conversation from his front row seat.

"Trey, let's hear what you have so far."

Her smile has vanished, replaced by her usual stern, pursed lips. I silently thank Mrs. Monroe for drawing the attention away from me and centering it on Trey, whose face is now as red as a cherry.

With Trey being much more entertaining to watch than me, not one person looks my way while I make it back to my seat and shove the paper down in my backpack.

Hopefully, she'll forget about this by tomorrow.

SHE DOESN'T FORGET.

Mrs. Monroe brings the contest up again—two days later.

At least it's not in front of the class this time. Instead, she catches me in the hall on my way to economics.

"Ms. Mancini!"

She'd just stepped out of the teacher's lounge, carrying a tall stack of copies balanced on one arm and a Dr Pepper in the other. I know what she's gonna say before the words come out of her mouth, so I beat her to the punch.

"Oh, hi, Mrs. Monroe. I haven't had the chance to look over that contest information yet."

I point to the Dr Pepper she's holding, attempting to knock her off the subject. "I didn't know you liked Dr Pepper. It's my favorite too."

She lifts it slightly and shakes her head.

"It's not my favorite." She grunts. "The staff vending machine is always out of Pepsi, and today was no exception."

Not to be deterred, she raises her eyebrows and says, "I really hope you take the time to look over the contest entry information, Alli. I believe you would have an excellent chance at placing. Even if you don't, it would be a valuable experience for you as a serious writer. You *are* serious about your writing, aren't you?"

The way she frames the question makes me cringe, as if writing the piece for the contest validates my claim to write anything, no matter the platform. Like, if I don't even make an attempt to write a story, I might as well hang up a sign on my bedroom wall that says *imposter* so I'll see it every time I sit to write anything for school or church. I'll look up, seeking inspiration, and the sign will remind me that I'm not a real writer because I never entered that contest that my English lit teacher recommended.

The sigh escapes before I even know it's coming. Partially because I'm afraid I could really be cursed with writer's block for all eternity and also because I'm about to make a painful confession to a teacher who put misguided faith in me.

"Oh, yes, writing is important to me. I've loved writing since I was a little kid, and I think I'm pretty good at it, but—"

"—You are," she interrupts.

I give her an appreciative nod.

"Thank you, but that's the thing. It's not that I don't think I can come up with something to write about, although I'm not sure it would be contest-worthy, but it's just that I don't *like* to write stories all that much."

I chance a look at her but can't read her expression.

"Sorry, I don't mean to let you down or anything," I say.

Her shoulders slump a fraction, but that could be because of the heavy stack of papers she's balancing on her arm.

"No, no, dear. Not at all. It was just a suggestion. You're a gifted writer, and I was just hoping to encourage you to step outside your comfort zone a little. Have you ever *tried* creative writing? Maybe you'd discover that you really enjoy creating fictional characters and venturing into genres you've never tried before."

I open my mouth to speak, but her glance toward the door stops me.

"You better get to class," she says. "It's my planning period, so I'm not in a hurry, but I wouldn't be late to class if you know what's good for you."

Her grin is infectious, and I read between the lines, both of us remembering butting heads when I was late to her class that fated morning.

Taking a step back, I make room for her to pass.

"Yes, ma'am, I wouldn't want that to happen."

Hearing her soft chuckle as she moves past me, I make a dash for my economics class, slipping in behind another student just in time.

Chapter Twenty-Eight

ANTHONY WALKS ME OUT TO MY CAR AFTER CHURCH.

I don't usually drive myself to church on Sunday mornings—preferring instead to save gas and ride with my parents—but I offered to cover the preschool Sunday school class this morning and needed to be at the church early to get things ready before the kids showed up.

I could tell that Anthony wasn't just walking me out to help load craft supplies in my trunk because he was way too chatty for his normal self.

Just from the preschool room all the way to my car in the middle of the parking lot, he'd made a comment about how he didn't remember preschoolers being so small, mentioned that one of the elders had recently bought a new truck and how that reminded him that he needed to change the oil in his own vehicle, and wondered aloud how

Jelly Belly had come up with over a hundred flavors of jelly beans.

Eyebrows raised, I give him a look from around the large box in my arms.

"Wow, that was random," I say.

When he laughs, I hear a tinge of nervous jitters under the surface.

He knows he isn't fooling me.

I pop the trunk open, and we unload our boxes. Feeling a little warm, I pull my jacket off and throw it on top of the stack. Then, I turn and give Anthony my most brilliant smile.

"Thanks, Anthony. You're the best."

Hands in pockets, he nods. "Sure. No problem."

I grin. "Anything else?"

He blinks.

"Uh, what do you mean? Did we forget something?"

He looks over his shoulder back toward the Sunday school room. When he looks back at me, I just stare, the brilliant smile still plastered on my face.

I'm kind of surprised that I'm being so coy because that's not my personality, but I guess I'm feeling braver than usual this morning. Maybe dealing with a room full of rowdy three- to five-year-olds all morning has empowered me with courage I didn't know I possessed.

It's his turn to grin.

He knows I've tagged him in.

Anthony's hands slide from his pockets as he reaches over and slams the trunk closed.

"Well, now that you mention it, there *is* something else."

Tilting my head, I wait. Of course, I know where this is going—and I already know my answer—but I don't let him off too easily.

"Would you like to go bowling Saturday night?"

Bowling? I think, as an unexpected stab of disappointment twists in my chest. I feel the corners of my smile melt into a straight line. I'd expected something—I don't know —more *romantic.*

But it's a start. At least, I guess it is.

Maybe he just wants to make it a fun night. I can live with that. Not wanting my face to betray my uncertainty, I force the corners of my mouth upward into a less-than-brilliant-but-convincing smile.

"Sure, um, that sounds great. What time?"

"Pick you up around 6:00?" he asks. "I'll check with your dad first, of course."

My dad?

For a second, my brain doesn't get the connection.

Is that normal? A guy asking my dad if he can take me out? Will Dad think Anthony's a nerd for asking his permission to take me . . . bowling?

I hate feeling so inexperienced and in the dark about this kind of stuff, but I don't want that fact to be too obvious. Maybe I'll ask Brynne to enlighten me tonight. She's more in the know about this kind of thing than me.

"Oh, yeah, sure, of course. Sounds good. Um, see you Saturday, then." I sputter and back up toward the driver door of the car, suddenly feeling bewildered.

The tables have turned, and I'm the one acting awkward while Anthony stands there looking relaxed and self-assured. I don't trust myself to say another word because I might end up saying something as random as his Jelly Belly comment.

"See you, Alli," he says, gives a small wave, and turns to leave.

I stand there watching him walk away, car keys hanging limp in my hand, and my heart doing somersaults in my throat.

Chapter Twenty-Nine

"Guess what?"

Tessa sounds more excited than I've heard her be in a while. It almost sounds like the old Tessa, and I feel my stomach leap, anticipation climbing into my chest.

"What?!"

I jump off the bed and run over to shut my bedroom door, almost dropping the phone when I trip over one of the throw pillows that had tumbled off the bed.

"You're not even gonna try to guess?" Her voice is playful, and it makes me smile.

"Um, you want to sneak out tonight and egg Mr. Ender's house?" I giggle.

Mr. Ender lives at the end of the block and is always sitting on his porch, scowling at anyone who comes within inches of his precious lawn. If you so much as put a big toe on his property, he rises from his chair and screams at you, one fist in the air. That sends his dog—an ugly pug that looks like it hasn't been bathed in a century—into a frenzy of barking. Between the old man and his dog, it's enough racket to disturb the dead.

Sometimes Tessa and I would watch for him and step onto his grass on purpose just to get him going, then take off running down the street.

I can hear Tessa snickering on the other end of the line.

"Old Mr. Ender," she says, wistfully. "I do kind of miss harassing him. I still see him sitting on his porch when Mom and I drive by and always think about how we tortured that poor old guy. Yeah, it *would* be fun to pay him a visit. But that's not it."

"Oh, alright, I give up. Tell me."

She makes me wait for several seconds, drawing out the suspense, before she announces with a squeal, "I passed my finals!"

At first it doesn't register, then it hits me at once.

"Ohhhh, your *finals*. Wow, Tessa, that's awesome!"

Being that Tessa only had a few months left of the school year, and she had gotten far behind, her teachers had worked out a system for her to finish her classes online. I knew she'd been working hard to catch up with the rest of us, but I honestly never believed she'd push through enough to finish on time.

"What did you think I was talking about, goofball?" she says.

I shake my head, even though she can't see it.

"I have no idea what I was thinking, but that's great! I know it was a lot of work to catch up. So . . ." I hesitate, not sure if I should bring it up. I worry that it's too soon.

"Does that mean you get to graduate with your class?" I ask.

Tessa doesn't answer for a moment, and I feel my heart thumping against my shirt.

Yep, it was too soon.

"Yeah," she finally says, and I'm relieved to hear that her enthusiasm is still intact. "I get to graduate on time, but I don't plan to go to the actual graduation ceremony or anything. I don't have any desire to ever go back there or see any of them, except maybe Shanice. She's cool. I just want to get my diploma and be done with it."

I let the mention of Shanice slide.

I outline the floral quilting on my blanket with my finger while I listen. I don't blame Tessa at all. She would have no peace if she actually showed up on graduation night. She'd be mauled by everyone asking her questions and telling her how sorry they are—or worse—saying nothing at all and giving her pitiful looks all night. And even worse than any of those scenarios would be them looking down their noses at her with disdain and judgment. It's everything Tessa *doesn't* need right now.

"Yeah," I say, "I get it."

Trying to keep things positive, I hurry past the moment.

"Wow. I'm so happy for you, Tessa. That's so amazing!"

"Thanks. It was tough for a while, but I'm glad I pushed through it," she says.

"So are you still planning to go to college?" I ask.

Ever since I can remember, Tessa had always planned to go to college to become a veterinarian, but I've felt so out of touch with her lately that I really don't know what her aspirations are anymore. We'd always joked that we had to attend the same college because I'd need Tessa to help me get through it.

Even though we didn't have the same goals for our careers, she kidded that we could at least be roommates and she'd crack the whip and make me study and do my homework. After that, when she was ready to move on to veterinarian school, I'd be on my own. I'd always joke back and say that I could just skip college and go work as a receptionist in her vet clinic when she opened her own practice.

Now I don't know if either one of us will end up going to college.

"I think so," she answers. "But not right away. I don't know . . . well, I'm not sure my parents would be able to afford it."

I sit up straighter on the bed, jumping to her defense because I've had this conversation with my advisor, Mrs. Arroyo.

"They have financial assistance available, Tessa, and grants. There are so many more options available—"

"—My grades aren't as stellar as they used to be, Alli," she interrupts. "I barely made it through my classes, and my testing scores weren't exactly . . . well, let's just say that none of the colleges will be beating down my door asking me to sign on with them. I've already thought about financial aid, but I need to meet with an advisor and see what my options are."

Tessa huffs in frustration. "I don't even know what college I'd *want* to look at and who'd even accept me. I'm late in even applying for the fall semester anyway." Her voice grows softer. "I'll probably end up at one of the community colleges to start with. I want to do as much as I can online."

"I get that," I say. "I think it's great that you're still wanting to go to college and all, even if you have to take a longer route to get there."

"Hmm, yeah, I guess," Tessa mumbles. "So have you applied at any of the colleges yet?"

My finger-tracing stops, and I rest my head back against my headboard, staring up at the ceiling, noticing how much my ceiling fan is in need of a good dusting.

"Um . . . I don't know yet. I'm still thinking about my options." I'm not really lying—I *am* still thinking, considering my options.

"Oh, got it," she says. "You could take a year off and think about it. Have you decided what you would major in if you do?"

I detect sadness in her tone, and, suddenly, I've lost interest in talking about college. As if I wasn't already struggling enough with the idea of leaving home and my church, the idea of leaving Tessa behind hits hard. We'd grown up planning to do what we've always done—stay together.

Does it really matter now? Haven't Tessa and I already steered onto opposite paths?

I know me moving to California would be the nail in the coffin for us. We'd get busy with our own lives, make new friends—which we've already started to do anyway—find new interests that don't involve each other, and maybe even fall in love, and who knows where it would all go from there.

When all was said and done, our paths would only cross if we met back here on our familiar turf, and that's a big *if.*

That train of thought brings Anthony to mind, although I'm not sure why. It's obvious that we're still figuring out where, if anywhere, our relationship might take us, and that means my move to California could extinguish that tiny flame as well.

"Journalism," I say abruptly, deciding not to elaborate.

"Yeah, I figured." She doesn't elaborate on my answer either.

Then she flips the conversation on its head with her next comment. If I wasn't expecting her announcement about passing finals and graduating, I certainly wasn't expecting this one.

"I was thinking of going to church this Sunday."

My head comes off the headboard. "Church? Really? Where?"

She knows she threw me a curveball and laughs.

"Yessss, church. You know, the building that has a steeple, and this guy stands behind a pulpit—"

"—Tessa!" I yell, and she laughs again.

"Well, I've only visited *one* other church—yours. I was thinking that I could just go . . . with you. I mean, if you don't care, that is."

Before I can say anything, she rushes in.

"Don't get all excited. I'm not going to get on God's good side or because it's a last resort for me. I just thought that, maybe, it might help me figure some things out, find some answers . . . I don't know."

My eyes blink, then blink again, and, before I know it, they start leaking, and I'm crying. Exactly in that order too. Only I don't want Tessa to know I'm crying because it might freak her out and make her change her mind. And I *don't* want her to change her mind.

I place a hand on my chest to steady myself and make sure my voice doesn't betray my emotions.

"Of course, Tessa! That would be great. I'd love for you to come with me on Sunday. Do you want to come by my house afterward for dinner? My mom's making meatball subs."

I know it's a cheap shot—the dinner invite—because Tessa loves my mom's meatball subs. Again, I don't want Tessa to change her mind, and I figure a little extra incentive can't hurt.

"The ones with mozzarella cheese dripping down them?" She says, and I know I've won her over.

"Yep, with homemade hoagie rolls and everything," I say, grinning like a coyote alone in a hen house.

"In that case—of course!"

We both laugh and spend the next few minutes finalizing our plans. It feels like we've both taken a step out onto the bridge between us and are taking baby steps toward each other.

I don't let my expectations get too high—after all, things will probably never be the same for us—but I do have a glimmer of hope.

Just the fact that Tessa was the one initiating a visit to church when it was always me nagging her to come in the past makes that hope glow just a little brighter.

Chapter Thirty

I INTRODUCE KRISTIN TO TESSA WHEN WE WALK INTO THE sanctuary, and, in true Kristin fashion, she pulls Tessa into a hug and her inner circle as if they'd known each other forever.

Kristin compliments Tessa's hair, spouts off a dorky joke, and even manages to give her a brief tour of the Sunday school rooms.

I start to give Kristin a look to let her know that she's overdoing it, but Tessa seems to enjoy the attention. I decide to kill the "overdoing it" look and let them be.

Brynne also welcomes Tessa warmly, but I can feel the apprehension on both their parts because of the past history they'd shared at school, and because Brynne knows how much Tessa had hurt me in the past. They'd probably need more time for the ice to thaw before there could be any real warmth between them.

The four of us sit together for church service, choosing to find a seat in the back instead of my normal place on the second row. It can get crowded on the front rows, and we don't want Tessa to feel overwhelmed.

I think it helps that other people stop by to greet Tessa and make her feel welcome. If any awkward silences or lulls in the conversation come up, one of the three of us agreed that we would step in to fill the void.

But there's no need for that because, by the end of the night, Tessa seems right at home. During service, we'd all giggled over Kristin's off-key singing and crammed our heads together to share Brynne's Bible when the minister read the opening scriptures since the rest of us had forgotten to bring a Bible.

We make plans to meet up the next night at a coffee shop to hang out. But when Brynne starts to bring up the weekly Bible studies we have with Anthony, I quickly change the subject. Brynne gives me a puzzled look but, thankfully, drops it.

When she excuses herself to go to the bathroom, I follow. Once we're alone, I remind Brynne about how Shanice and Kim have dropped in on our Bible studies before just to cause trouble. She's gracious about it, agreeing to save the invite for another time.

We end up going to Benji's Beans, one of my favorite coffee shops. Benji's was my suggestion for two reasons. One, they make an exceptional white chocolate mocha, and, two, it's not the most well-known place in town and I figured we were less likely to run into anyone we knew there.

Tessa hasn't left her house much over the past several months, and I know that being out in public still makes her feel anxious. When we arrive, I lead the way, seeking out the most secluded table I can find.

I spy the perfect place in the rear corner of the shop, a booth surrounded on three sides by crowded bookshelves. If I wanted to hide from the world and read in a quiet location, that table would be the ideal spot.

Come to think of it, it would also be the perfect spot to rally for planning a covert military operation, but that's just my overactive imagination kicking in.

As we file toward the corner, Brynne glances over at the barista standing at an espresso machine off to our right. I tap Brynne on the shoulder.

"Let grab the table and then we'll order. I'll buy Tessa's."

My offer is more to allow Tessa to remain at the table out of sight than the fact that I'm being generous.

"Okay." Brynne nods. "Sounds good."

Benji's Beans looks like it passed its prime back in the 70s. Bright yellow and orange tablecloths drape across round tables, and ivory macrame plant holders hang in two corners, vines with sparse leaves covered in a gray layer of dust cascading down from each one.

On our way to the table, my gaze runs over a ceramic plate arrangement on one wall, each plate painted with pixie-faced children with big eyes and short, tight hairstyles that remind me of the Beatles.

Situating ourselves around the table, a familiar scent drifts my way that reminds me of my Nonno Mancini. Hints of cinnamon and bitter orange fill my nostrils, and I'm transported to Nonna and Nonno's old house and the familiar fragrance that clung to the bathroom towels and drifted up from the numerous throw rugs Nonna kept throughout the house.

It takes me a moment to identify it: Old Spice.

My Nonno kept a large bottle of it on the shelf in the guest bathroom. For a long time, I thought it was room fragrance until I watched my Nonno spritz himself from the bottle one morning after he shaved.

Brynne nudges me, breaking my nostalgic trance.

"Ready to go order?" she says.

She doesn't bother asking Kristin, knowing she doesn't drink coffee and is already pulling a water bottle out of her purse.

I nod and slip my wallet out of my bag. Leaning close to Tessa, I whisper, "My treat. You want a caramel latte?"

Her eyes glow with happiness, and I wonder how long it's been since she's done anything fun outside of the house before tonight. Tessa used to live for her coffee, and the gratitude on her face tells me this is just what she needed.

"Thanks! I'd love that. Extra whipped cream, too, please."

I smile. "You got it."

Brynne's already giving her order to the barista when I approach and start looking at the chalkboard sign above the register with the drink menu handwritten in perfect block letters. I browse the list and see flavors like raspberry macadamia chocolate and a Thai iced coffee with fresh vanilla bean.

When Brynne steps aside to let me order, I still haven't decided what I want.

"Um, I'll take an iced white chocolate mocha," I say, sticking with the familiar. "Medium, please. Oh, and another medium hot caramel latte with extra whip."

When we arrive back at the table, I slide the hot latte over to Tessa and watch as she takes a tentative sip.

"Ahhhh." She swallows. "Perfect." She pokes me with a playful finger. "Thanks."

Shaking my head, I say, "No problem. Enjoy."

"So are guys ready for graduation?" Kristin's gaze fall on each of us, settling on Tessa last. Her eyes widen when she realizes her mistake. But Tessa doesn't allow time for awkwardness before she shares her news.

"Yeah, I am."

All eyes are on Tessa now, and I give her an encouraging smile, sharing in the joy of her recent accomplishment. She shrugs and looks down at her cup, tracing a finger around the edge of the lid.

"I passed my finals. But I . . . um, I won't be attending the actual graduation ceremony or anything. And I'm not sure yet about college," she finishes in a quiet voice.

Brynne finds her voice first.

"That's great, Tessa! I'm so ready to be done with high school. I'm super excited about college but kinda nervous too. I've gotten my acceptance letter from University of Florida."

"Florida?" Tessa asks.

"Yeah," Brynne says. "My grandparents live there and I can save money by staying with them. Besides, I'm thinking of getting my pharmacy degree, and UF has a good program."

Kristin recovers and jumps in.

"I'm just taking my general ed classes at the local community college for starters. I hope to transfer to a Bible college in Indiana after that."

Kristin has always been homeschooled, and, in some ways, her mom was stricter on her than any of our public-school teachers. I'm positive she'll survive just fine in college.

The conversation lulls, and I catch Kristin looking my way.

"What about you, Alli?"

I glance at Brynne because I've already had this conversation with her. I hesitate, reluctant to say anything in front of Tessa because I *haven't* had this conversation with her yet.

I don't know why it matters either.

It's not like we've had a lot of opportunities for my future plans to come up in our conversations. But, after being fragile for so many months, I'm watching the beginning of the butterfly coming out of the cocoon. I'm afraid to disrupt the process or set her back because, well, what if she *does* care?

Well, here we go.

"I'm applying to the University of Southern California," I say. "For journalism."

"You're moving to California?" Tessa stares at me, her face a mask of confusion and shock.

"Yeah, sure, that's the plan, but, uh, I haven't even finished the application process yet," I say, brushing it off like it's no big deal.

"You will, Alli, if I have to come to your house and fill it out myself," Brynne tags in.

Then, looking at Tessa, she adds, "Especially if she can get that internship with that magazine."

Tessa's eyes widen. "An internship?"

If I could curl into a ball and roll under the table without anyone noticing, I would. I realize that Brynne probably assumes that I've shared all this with Tessa already, but I haven't—on purpose.

Truthfully, I haven't even decided that I'm ready for all the changes yet. Sure, it's been my dream and would be the perfect opportunity to get out of Tucson and try something new, but making it public wasn't yet on my agenda. I catch Brynne's eye and shake my head. She looks confused for a second, then understanding sinks in.

Sorry, she mouths.

Kristin pipes in, unaware of the sudden unease.

"Really? I hadn't heard anything about an internship. Do tell!"

Avoiding Tessa's eyes, I focus on Kristin, knowing I'll be addressing Tessa's curiosity as well.

"I applied for an intern position at a Christian publication. It would be a great opportunity to get my foot in the door and learn the ropes. I haven't heard back from them yet though."

I raise my cup and take a big gulp of coffee.

"It's a super competitive internship, so I'm not getting my hopes up too much about it."

I notice Tessa opening her mouth to say something, but I cut her off before she does.

"Brynne has some great news to share too," I say, swinging the attention to Brynne and away from me.

Brynne looks stunned for a moment before realizing what I mean.

"Oh," she says, the corners of her mouth lifting. "Yeah, it's been a lot of hard work but worth it."

No one at the table but me knows what she's talking about, so I have to fill the others in. I drum my index fingers on the table for an intro.

"Introducing . . . West Morrison High School's valedictorian! Yay!"

Kristin starts clapping right away while Tessa still looks shell-shocked from all the information coming at her at lighting speed. I know she's still processing my announcement before she absorbs any of the others.

"Wow, that's great, Brynne," she finally manages to squeak out.

I feel bad for using Brynne as my scapegoat, especially since I know Tessa probably could've been a runner-up herself as smart as she is and how fantastic her grades were. She'd lost out on another senior-year experience once again, and I can't help but get the sense that this whole conversation is one big blunder.

Wondering how I can redeem our time together and shift things back to safer ground, I blurt out the first thing that comes to mind.

"Not to change the subject," I say, although that's *exactly* what I'm attempting to do, "but Avery's got a boyfriend."

Three sets of curious eyes turn to me.

"A *boyfriend?*" Kristin asks. "Isn't she a little young?"

I start to giggle and tap a finger on my chin.

"Yes, ma'am. His name is Jake, and he's in her music class. She complains that he follows her around at recess and lunch, but I think she really likes it. She claims that he's always bumping her chair on purpose in class and throwing erasers and paper wads at her."

I sigh and fan myself with my hand. "Oh, isn't young love divine?"

Tessa giggles behind her napkin, and I'm relieved to have thwarted the topic of my future plans—if they *are* still my plans. Brynne and Kristin join in the laughter.

"There was this neighbor boy when I was thirteen," Kristin starts. She looks upward, brows furrowed. "Hmm, what was his name again?" She chews on her lip. "Oh, yeah, Brody! Anyhow, he used to kick his soccer ball over the fence a few times a week just to talk to me. I knew that's why he was doing it because the ball only came over when I happened to be in the back yard doing something and he knew I was there. He wouldn't even come knock on our door to ask either. He'd just pop his head over our fence and ask me to toss it back over. I mean, what if I had been sunbathing or something?"

Kristin throws her hands in the air and we all crack up.

"Think about it," she continues. "Imagine a ball flying into your yard and then some guy's face popping up over the fence a minute later. He totally creeped me out."

"Okay, that *is* super weird," Brynne agrees. "You should've kept the ball and told him he could knock on the door and get it from your dad. That would have solved the problem real quick."

"Nah." Kristin waves a hand in the air. "He and his family ended up moving to Minnesota two years ago. A young couple with twin girls live there now. The girls, Sadie and Sommer, are three years old and super cute. But they have this little dog—some breed with long hair that makes him look like a mop—that barks constantly. It drives my mom insane. But I'll take annoying dogs over peeping neighbor boys any day."

After the clumsy start, we end up having a great time together.

We laugh as Brynne demonstrates her yodeling skills,

earning glares from a couple seated at a table nearby, and tease Kristin about being the only one of us who can roll her tongue. Tessa ends up laughing so hard at one point that she spills hot coffee on herself and almost pulls the tablecloth off the table when she jumps out of her chair.

I'm positive that everyone would agree that our girls' night out was a success.

We all make a promise to get out together more often. I look at the four of us in wonder, amazed that four girls from very different backgrounds and personalities have clicked so well.

I drive Tessa home.

It's a first for us because Tessa had always been the one driving us around because I didn't have a car. She still has her car but asked if I wouldn't mind driving tonight. I agreed. Tessa says she prefers to walk home from my house since she lives just a few houses down. We pull up in my driveway, and I turn the car off. But neither of us makes a move to get out.

"Thanks for the ride, Alli. And for the coffee date. It was a lot of fun," Tessa says with a grateful smile.

Her smile is contagious.

"You're welcome. I had a lot of fun too," I say.

We're both quiet for a moment, digesting our evening together in silence.

"I'm glad you came, Tessa. I really am," I say.

Her face grows serious. "Same here. I'm glad I went too."

Satisfied that there's nothing else to say on the topic, Tessa reaches down and picks up my purse, admiring it. I tell her it's a used Coach purse I found at Goodwill a few weeks ago.

"No way! How much?" She asks, not shy about inspecting all the pockets and digging inside.

I wink when I inform her that it only cost me twelve dollars because it was a red-tag day and was half off.

"Great deal," she mutters, holding the purse up by the handles to admire it.

"Next week is a yellow-tag sale," I tell her. "Wanna go with me?"

I see the warmth in her expression when she looks over at me. Thrift shopping and yard sales were Tessa and my favorite things to do together.

Back when we were still acting like best friends, that is.

Tessa doesn't know it, but she's still mine, even if we haven't called each other "best friends" for a long time. Even after all we've been through and the times I almost hated her, I could never fully strip that title from her.

But, again, Tessa doesn't know that. Perhaps I'll tell her someday.

She hesitates before answering. "Uh, let me think about it."

I realize that I might be asking too much of Tessa right now, and I'm okay with that. She can take all the time she needs.

She opens the car door but doesn't step out yet. Instead, she turns to me with a timid smile.

"Are you really moving away, Alli? To college and all that?"

I swallow the lump in my throat and stare out past the windshield, out over the quiet street dimly lit by porch lights, the yellow streetlights soon to follow.

Just the fact that Tessa's asking me that question—that she *cares* about losing me—is what causes me to choke up. A month ago, I'd been almost convinced of moving. I dragged my feet because I was afraid of the unknown, but I had felt more positive each day that my future led to some place far from Tucson. But now that Tessa asks the question, none of it feels right anymore.

I turn my attention back to her.

"I don't know, Tessa. I thought I did, but I just don't know yet."

She nods but doesn't press for more.

"Thanks again, Alli. I really enjoyed church yesterday and, you know, hanging out with everyone tonight."

"Me too, Tessa."

I sit and watch her walk down the sidewalk, see her turn around and wave, then turn toward her house. A moment later, she disappears behind the big tree in her yard.

I stay in the car, allowing the solitary moment to calm my senses and give my body time to catch up with my spirit.

This also feels like a good a time to have a talk with God.

Chapter Thirty-One

"I DON'T BELONG HERE, GOD. YOU KNOW THAT."

The intensity of my voice in the small space of the car catches me by surprise.

I fidget with the straps of my purse, winding them around my fingers, and stare at the vacated passenger's seat. I still can't believe Tessa had just been sitting there a few minutes ago. I also can't believe she'd initiated the visit to church and that we'd hung out at the coffee shop tonight. It was almost like old times.

Church. Wow.

After all these years of me begging her to go. Sure, she'd come a time or two when we'd had fun youth nights, like playing volleyball or going to harvest festivals, but she'd always found a way to turn me down when it came to a regular church service with worship and preaching involved.

"Nah, your church is too weird," she'd tease, but I think she really felt that way deep down. "I love you, Alli," she would tell me. "But I don't see why you have to dress and act so differently. There are loads of people who are Christians who don't have to go all out like you do."

Tessa even joked with me once saying that I belonged to a cult. She told me, "You're my best friend for always, Alli, but let's agree to never talk about religion, okay?"

And I had honored that.

Except for a few rare occasions, religion wasn't a topic we discussed.

Once, when Tessa's grandmother was sick in the hospital, I told her I'd pray for her. Tessa nodded gratefully and didn't reject the offer. Whether it was as a result of prayer or not, her grandmother recovered. Tessa didn't attribute the outcome to God or to fate. For Tessa, religion wasn't something that was necessary. My promise to pray for her grandmother was, in her way of thinking, just the standard token people offer when hearing of others' misfortunes.

And so, the vast differences that Tessa and I had between us were brushed under the rug.

She knew I had boundaries and respected them, only challenging me a few times to cross them, which, unfortunately, I did way more often than I'm proud of.

It was just a matter of time before other people began shouting those differences from the rooftops, and, suddenly, Tessa's tolerance of my faith was challenged through the eyes of others who *couldn't* tolerate it.

She could no longer turn a blind eye to them and salvage her own reputation. The friendship Tessa and I shared wasn't strong enough to keep her from cutting the cord and distancing herself from me as far as she could.

I wipe at a stray tear and turn my eyes heavenward.

"Tessa never claimed to be anyone different than who she was, God, and that's what she lived. Yet I profess to be a Christian but agreed to lock my faith in a box and set it on a shelf to avoid offense," I sob.

The guilt of this revelation is like the weight of a mountain on my shoulders, and it's several moments before I can control my weeping and go on.

"That's all the more reason for me to leave here, God. To start over with a blank slate. I haven't always been the best example to Tessa and the others at school, and maybe I haven't been as vocal and willing to share you with them, but I did try to live what I believe."

A car passes by and I quickly duck my head, worried that someone might think I'm talking to myself and question my sanity or sobriety. Then, I consider that I'm in my driveway, facing the house, and it's now dark outside.

No one can see me in here, I assure myself.

Reaching up to tuck a loose strand of hair behind my ear, I end up wiping at the fresh tears on my cheek instead.

I think of my parents, Avery, my youth group . . . Anthony. I'd miss them if I left. All of them. I have so many cherished memories here in Tucson. Sure, I'd visit often, but it wouldn't feel the same. I'd be an outsider.

And Anthony? I can't deny that there is something happening between us. And although it is still just a spark, with time it could fan into something brighter.

Would I always wonder what I had walked away from if I don't give it—give us—a chance? Would Anthony feel the same disappointment if I left the spark to smolder into cold ashes?

My heart hurts thinking of leaving and what I might lose. But my heart hurts just the same when I consider staying. There's no peace for me no matter which road I choose.

"Why won't you show me what to do, God? Why is this so hard?"

I sit quietly, emotionally spent.

I stay like that for a few more minutes just in case God decides to answer while he has my undivided attention. But, after those few minutes, the silence makes me restless and I'm ready to call it a night.

"I'm waiting on you now, God," I say and step out of the car.

Chapter Thirty-Two

"Let's play *Guess Alli's Crush*," Brynne teases.

The look on my face just feeds the fire.

"Oh, come on, Alli, don't think the rest of us haven't noticed."

Tessa giggles. "Oh, I know," she says. "It's definitely Zach. No doubt about it."

I throw my hands up and glare at Tessa. "*Zach?*"

"Oh, for sure! Why hadn't I noticed?" Brynne says. "I was wondering why she's suddenly so interested in science and is always asking Zach if she can borrow his notes."

My head spins around to Brynne.

"What are you talking about? I never ask Zach for his science notes!"

Brynne and Tessa double over with laughter.

I'm incredulous.

"I don't like Zach!" I grab for the closest object within reach—an empty box of Whoppers that we'd polished off—and chuck it at Brynne. She catches it before it hits her and throws it back.

"Fine," Brynne says, turning to Tessa. "Zach's out. Try another guess."

Tessa smiles and gives me a sly look.

"Like we haven't all known for years that it would be Anthony," she says.

"Awww . . ." The two of them croon in harmony.

Brynne and Tessa both stare at me with puppy-dog eyes and hands crossed over their hearts.

I feel my cheeks flush, but I don't dare crack a smile and give myself away. If I did, the two of them would pounce on me with their teasing, like dogs on a bone.

But inside my chest, my heart is doing cartwheels and swinging on the monkey bars.

Brynne's grin turns territorial. "So, Alli, do you want to tell her, or should I?"

Tessa scoots to the end of her seat. "Tell me what?"

Brynne's referring to my unofficial date with Anthony.

I don't know, does going bowling translate to a real date? I still haven't settled that in my mind yet.

I'd always thought official dates involved flowers at the door and candles on the table of a fancy restaurant. Anthony and I had a lot of fun—a *lot* of fun—bowling, but we didn't make eyes at each other all night or finish each other's sentences. Still, we *did* have our share of flirting comments the whole time.

I don't realize that I'm smiling until Brynne nudges me.

"Alli?" Brynne prods, then looks over at Tessa. "Do you see the smile on this girl's face?"

Tessa claps her hands together in glee. "Oh, do tell, Alli . . . Brynne . . . *somebody*."

"We went bowling," I sputter. "We were, you know, hanging out."

"Hanging out?" Tessa says, one eyebrow raised. "Like, *alone*? Just you and *him*?"

Brynne pats Tessa on the shoulder.

"Oh, they were alone alright. And, if you know Anthony at all, he doesn't just *hang out* with girls. He's always been smitten with our Alli, but the poor girl has been clueless. He even asked her dad before he took her out, like a proper gentleman. I think Mr. Mancini was smiling as big as Alli is right now."

She turns to me and smirks.

"Yes, Tessa and I would be flattered to be in your wedding. Thanks for asking."

Tessa and Brynne hoot with laughter while I look on, letting them have their moment.

It's not like I was clueless, as Brynne put it. I knew Anthony kind of liked me, and I'd caught him staring at me more than once. You'd think after being with Chad that I'd know what a date looks like, but, for some reason, being with Anthony feels like uncharted territory. Everything feels different when I'm around him.

He's always been someone I looked up to—the responsible one, the conscientious, above-board, godly example that put the rest of us in the youth group to shame—so much that I guessed he'd never look twice at me. The girl who lived on the fringes of a true relationship with God, who dabbled with the dangerous on occasion, and who barely masked her boredom during youth services.

Why me? I wonder.

"Earth to Alli," Tessa says. "Are you even here right now, or is your head still in the clouds?"

My shoulders droop as I chew on my bottom lip.

"It was just one date, you guys. I don't know if he'll even ask me out again. Maybe he was just wanting to get to know me better. That doesn't make us a couple or anything."

"Well, what did he say when he took you home at the end of the night?" Brynne asks.

I start picking at strands of the carpet in front of me, avoiding her gaze.

"He said he had a good time and that we should . . . do it again soon," I finish lamely, knowing I've been backed into a corner.

"Um, unless I misunderstood you when you mentioned it the other day," Brynne says, "you told me he said he had a *great* time."

I roll my eyes. "Ok, he said a *great* time."

"Oh, yep. It's official. They're gonna have a second date," Tessa gushes.

This time, I find an empty soda bottle within reach and lunge it at Tessa.

I STOP by Mrs. Monroe's class and see her sitting alone at her desk. Tapping gently on the door, I wait for her to notice me. She looks up and waves me in.

"Alli, my girl! Come on in. What can I do for you?"

I smile and make my way over to her desk. Pointing at the photo of the two little tan and white Yorkshire Terriers, I ask, "How's Mitzi?"

The only other thing Mrs. Monroe loves more than teaching English lit is her two Yorkies, Mitzi and Fritz.

She can be right in the middle of talking about a dark scene from the novel *Of Mice and Men* and, with just the right prompting from a student, launch into a cute story about one of her dogs. Even though she knows we're trying to distract her on purpose, she never seems to mind spending a few stray minutes telling us about her fur babies.

Mrs. Monroe had recently shared with the class that one of her dogs, Mitzi, had broken her leg when she fell off the side of the porch. Since the class has heard about Mitzi and Fritz the whole school year, we can't help but become invested in them too.

"Oh," Mrs. Monroe laughs. "She's fit as a fiddle but is

really taking advantage of all the attention she's getting. I know she starts limping the minute I walk into the room just so I'll lift her onto my lap for a cuddle. Fritz gets so jealous too! He sits and moans and growls up at Mitzi on my lap and won't even touch his treat."

I laugh and walk over to set my backpack down on a nearby desk. As I unzip the bag and pull out my black binder, I say, "I'm glad Mitzi is doing better. Fritz will just have to get over it."

"Indeed, he will," Mrs. Monroe says.

Opening the binder, I pull three neatly typed pages from a folder. I walk over to Mrs. Monroe and set the papers down in front of her.

"What's this?" she asks, picking the papers up and scanning them.

"My story. For the writing contest."

Her face brightens, and she beams up at me.

"Why, Alli, I'm so glad you decided to enter!" She flips through the papers and returns them to her desk. "Do you still have the entry form?" she asks.

I cringe and give her a guilty look. "I lost it. Would you happen to have another one?"

She smiles and nods.

"I can print another copy. We can fill it out this afternoon and submit it right away. The closing date is in three days."

"Okay, sounds good," I say. "I better head to class. Thanks for your time, Mrs. Monroe."

She nods and turns her attention back to the papers, settling in to read.

"You're welcome, Alli. Good luck."

Pulling my backpack off the desk, I shrug it onto my shoulder and slip from the room.

Now if I can just get the piece about Brynne finished.

Chapter Thirty-Three

I feel an elbow in my right side for the third time and growl into the ear of the girl next to me.

"Kristin, if you don't scoot over and give me more room, I'm gonna jam my heel down on your foot."

I feel her squirm, but her body remains smashed against mine.

"I can't. Brynne's rear end is taking up the whole space," she whispers back.

Brynne overhears the remark and pretends she's getting something out of her purse on the floor, so no one sees her talking.

"It's not my rear end that's the problem, Kristin. Your suitcase is hogging up half the pew. You're not too good to put your purse on the floor like the rest of us, you know."

I'm attempting to stare straight ahead, but from my

peripheral vision, I see Kristin's head shaking back and forth.

"Ewww, no. My purse—it's not a *suitcase*, thank you—is white, and that," she motions to the floor, "is where people put their feet. Who knows the last time they had these carpets cleaned?"

Tessa jabs her elbow into my left side.

"Will you guys be quiet? That old guy is looking over here, and he doesn't look happy."

We fix our eyes back to the front, where Brother Terrell, the assistant pastor, is delivering a long-winded sermon. It's no wonder we're getting antsy shoved up against each other in this pew.

Brynne starts to dig in her purse again. While we do our best to ignore her, it's a welcome distraction at this point. But when her purse dumps over and the contents spill onto Kristin's feet, all four of us start giggling, faces turning red while we try desperately to hold back the ripples of laughter that threaten to overcome us. Brynne laughs the hardest, but she's also still leaned over in the pew and can hide it better.

I'm positive the Perkins family seated behind us are wondering what all the commotion is about.

We're barely containing ourselves—the pew trembles under our shaking bodies. I'm stuck in the middle, so there's no easy way for me to escape to the bathroom. I haven't had a fit of giggles in church like this since Charlene Spencer and I had a pinching contest on the front pew when we were kindergarteners waiting for our Sunday school class to be called up to sing for Mother's Day.

It feels good to be sitting beside Tessa in public again. And to be sitting beside her in church is more than I could have hoped for in a million years.

Tessa hasn't decided how she feels about God yet, but she asks lots of questions and has been coming to church regularly for a few weeks now. I take that as a good sign that she's on the right track, and I'm proud of how far she's come in her healing process.

We talk about a lot of deep things when we're together, more than we have since she first came home from New Mexico. Sometimes we end up crying, and I think that's a good thing too.

Tessa has also accepted Brynne as part of our besties trio, and we hang out with each other a lot.

But Tessa allows only me access to the most private parts of her life and the secrets she's borne for a long time. Her therapist says that I've been good for her, but I think the benefit is mutual. Tessa's been good for me too. She's taught me about what matters and what doesn't.

About *who* matters and *who* doesn't.

I told her about Shanice and how sad she looks these days. Believe it or not, it was Tessa who suggested we pray for Shanice, and Brynne couldn't have agreed more.

So I do. I pray for Shanice almost every day and even make it a point to say a few nice words to her when we cross paths.

In fact, this last Friday, I even felt brave enough to sit by her during lunch. Brynne was a little surprised and even hesitated for a second before agreeing to join me. Shanice didn't say much after we sat down, but I could tell she seemed glad that we were there, even moving her designer purse over to make room for me to sit next to her. If someone had been following the history between Shanice and me this school year, they'd have no doubt that miracles are possible.

I'm so lost in my thoughts that I don't even notice that everyone around me is standing. I jump to my feet, smoothing down my dress so no one notices the flush of embarrassment on my face. I hear a crunch under my shoe and tilt slightly back from the pew to look down. Lifting my shoe, I see Brynne's lip balm canister cracked down the middle on the carpet. I can't resist a giggle before kicking it under the pew.

Kristin gives me a nudge. "Don't start again," she growls, but I hear the smile in her voice.

When Brother Terrell dismisses the congregation, the four of us make a beeline for the fellowship hall, where we know nachos are being served. Of course, we'll let the elders be served before us, but we plan to be in line right behind them, even though it takes them forever to make their way to the hall.

Just as we reach the double doors leading out of the sanctuary, Anthony glides up and opens one of the doors for us, beaming like an overzealous firefly in a dark cave.

"Hey, Alli," he says, and it's not lost on me that he only greets me and not the other young ladies I'm walking with.

"Heyyyy, Alli," Brynne coos behind me. Thankfully, she's not loud enough for Anthony to hear.

"Hey, Anthony. Thanks," I say and am rewarded with a beaming smile.

I step through the door and turn to wait for Brynne, Kristin, and Tessa. Kristin and Tessa greet Anthony with a mumbled thank you, but Brynne can't leave it alone.

"What's up, Anthony?" She says brightly.

Brynne smiles up at Anthony, but her eyes dart between me and him, and she isn't subtle about it. If Tessa hadn't felt so new and awkward, she would have been right there with Brynne, making a show out of the whole thing.

"Nothin' much," he replies, nodding to Brynne once, then glancing over at me, like he's trying to figure out if Brynne's sending some kind of a telepathic message between us that he can't decipher.

All of us girls stand on the other side of the door Anthony is still holding open, blocking the doorway and looking like the group of gawky teenage girls that we are. If it weren't for two ladies from the church waiting to get through, who knows how long we'd have stood there swapping confused looks back and forth.

I move close to Brynne and tug on her sweater sleeve to encourage her to move on. She barely scoots aside and lets the ladies brush past her before tilting her head back up to Anthony.

"Soooo, are you staying for nachos, Anthony?"

She looks back at me, and I see *that* look on her face. The one that tells me that she's about to do something she won't regret at all, but that I probably will.

I shake my head subtly, and, once again, she ignores me.

"Uh, I'm not sure yet," he says, glancing past her to me. "Why?"

Brynne reaches back and wraps an arm around my shoulder. I want to kick her.

"Oh, well, poor Alli's stomach was growling the whole service. I'm sure people three pews away could hear it."

Kristin and Tessa are loving the show. They stand off to the side, blending in with the crowd of people gathering in the foyer, snorting and giggling behind their Bibles while Brynne has her fun. Meanwhile, I melt into a horrified puddle behind her.

However, Anthony doesn't seem to mind at all. His eyebrows raise, and he nods my way.

"Well, we can't let Alli starve, can we?"

I shove Brynne's arm off of me and tug on her sleeve, much harder this time.

"That's super kind of you," I burst out, "but I'm nowhere close to *starving*," I say, giving Anthony my most charming smile, then shooting a death look at Brynne.

"Brynne," I say, "Why don't we all head over to the fellowship hall for nachos . . . *like we planned?*"

I notice Tessa, Brynne, and Kristin exchange looks.

Suddenly, the three of them spin around and head toward the bathroom, leaving me standing alone in front of Anthony.

Something tells me that none of them has to go to the bathroom.

Anthony holds the door for an elderly gentleman before letting the door close and stepping closer to me. His hands are in his pockets. I notice he does that a lot. It must be a nervous habit.

"I say you and I dump them and go grab something to eat somewhere else," he says with a wink and a nod toward the exit. I look toward the exit, then up at Anthony.

"Are you serious?"

"Yep." By the look on his face, I can tell he is.

Glancing toward the bathroom, I don't see any sign of the conniving trio. They must be stalling in there on purpose.

I spy my dad talking to a group of men just outside the front doors and turn my attention back to Anthony.

"You're on. Let me ask my dad."

The way Anthony's eyes light up, I know I've made the right decision.

"I'll ask him, if that's okay," he says, ever the gentleman. He glances over to the bathroom, where the girls still haven't emerged.

Leaning close, he whispers, "Let's hurry."

Dad gives his permission, a broad grin on his face. I can tell Anthony's interest in me makes him happy.

Just as we head out to the parking lot where Anthony's truck is parked, a family makes their way out of the front doors, and I see the girls standing in the foyer looking around for me. I quicken my pace to match Anthony's, and we make it to his truck. It's dark outside, except for a few yellow, fluorescent lights dotting the parking lot.

Unlocking the truck, Anthony opens my door first, and I shuffle into the passenger seat. He runs around to the driver's side, hops in, and snaps his seatbelt on.

We're almost out of the parking lot when I see Tessa come around the corner of the building, Brynne and Kristin in her wake.

This time, it's Anthony and me who burst out laughing at the looks on their faces as he taps on his horn and I wave at them through the truck window.

Chapter Thirty-Four

I WAS EXPECTING THE SOFT TAP ON MY DOOR LONG BEFORE it came.

But what I wasn't expecting was for Mom to wait to be invited in instead of just opening the door like she normally does.

Oh, now she decides to respect my privacy, after years of me complaining about her barging in all the time, I think.

But I don't really mean it. Part of me feels sad about the change in our comfortable routine.

"Come in."

The door opens slowly, and Mom slips in so quietly that, if I hadn't been watching her, I would've never known she was in here. She blinks to adjust her eyes to the dimness of the room.

"Why are you sitting in the dark?" she says as she makes her way to where I'm sitting on the bed.

I reach over and flip the switch for the lamp on my nightstand. A soft glow falls over the bed.

"I was on my phone. I didn't notice that it was getting dark in here."

She glances around the room before lowering herself onto the bed next to me. Her gaze takes in the room before settling on the three bulky shadows against the far wall.

"Oh, you have everything packed already." There are elements of both surprise and sadness in her voice.

"No, not yet. I haven't even started. Dad took the few boxes I had and put them in the garage. There's nothing in them that I need right now."

I motion toward the suitcases by the wall. "I had him bring those up so I could start packing."

I look from the suitcases to her stricken face.

"I'm not leaving for a few weeks, Mom. I just wanted to have them so I could start figuring out what clothes I'm taking and what stays here."

She nods but doesn't look at me right away. When she does, I see the mist in her eyes.

"Mom?"

She reaches out and rubs my knee, a gesture of comfort she's done since I was a little girl. Right now, I don't know if the gesture is for my benefit or if she's trying to comfort herself.

I pat the empty place next to me and smile. She returns the smile and scoots herself across the bed and up against the headboard, pressing gently against my side. I lay my head on her shoulder.

"Do you want me to stay home?" I ask, a half-hearted attempt at humor.

"Yes," she says.

I pop my head up to look at her. She reaches up and pushes my head back to her shoulder.

"No, of course not. I want this opportunity for you. We've prayed about it together and talked about it for months. I know this is a good thing, and I'm very happy for you, Alli."

I wiggle my arm behind her and hug her waist. I feel her hand wrap around mine.

"But . . .?"

I know there's more she isn't saying.

"But . . ." she pauses, "it's not easy for me—the letting go part. I'm sending my daughter off to the unknown, and I can't help but worry about all the challenges you will face. Challenges that I won't be there for."

"You'll be a phone call away, Mom. You know I'll be calling you about everything. You can't get rid of me that easily."

"I know," she says, and I feel the weight of her doubt and sadness through my head on her shoulder. I feel like crying, but I won't do that to her. We'll have plenty of time for the emotions later.

"How's Avery handling it? Don't you dare let her talk you into giving her my room," I say.

Her body shakes with laughter.

"Oh, she's already asking," Mom says with a chuckle. "But," her tone becomes serious, "she's having a harder time with you leaving than I am on some days."

Mom rubs her thumb across the top of my hand. "Maybe you could spend some extra time with her before you leave."

"I'll invite her for a sleepover in my room this weekend. Maybe we could do face masks and have a pizza delivered."

"Oh, would that be *me* delivering pizza?" She asks.

"Yep. How nice of you to offer, Mom."

It feels good to hear Mom laugh.

She playfully shoves my head off her shoulder and jabs a finger into my side, causing me to shriek and pull back. Scooting off the bed, she looks back at me, her eyes soft and loving.

"I love you, Allisandra. I'm going to miss you like crazy and I'll be counting down the days until you come home for a visit. But I know you'll do just fine in California."

I thought I was gonna hold off on the crying, but hearing Mom address me by my full name like Nonna used to do is too much for me. I allow for one small tear.

"I'll miss you too, Mom. Dad and Avery too." I sniff, then make an attempt at humor to ease the pain. "When I'm a famous journalist someday, I'll send home fat checks and take you guys on trips with me around the world."

I can still hear her laughter from behind the closed door

after Mom leaves. I'm relieved that she left in a much lighter mood than she'd come in with.

I can't help but laugh too.

"Famous journalist," I snort. "Yeah, right."

Chapter Thirty-Five

My cell phone rings when I'm in the shower.

I have to wait until I dry off to see who it was. Tapping on the screen, I see that I've missed a call from Brynne. I tap her contact and hit speaker phone so I can talk while I'm getting dressed.

"Eek! I love it!" she squeals.

"Hey yourself!" My voice is muffled under the shirt I'm attempting to pull over my head. When my head pops out, I grin at myself in the mirror. I know exactly what Brynne is referring to.

"You made me sound like I'm in line for the next presidential election. Girl, reading this article, I almost believe West Morrison High has never had a better student than Brynne Patterson. West Morrison's valedictorians for years to come will have a tough act to follow. Thanks, Alli."

"Awww, you're welcome, Brynne," I say. "And you *are*

gonna be a hard act to follow. This high school hasn't seen the likes of Brynne Patterson in its history."

She laughs. "My favorite part is when you quoted me as saying . . ." I hear paper crinkling in the background and know she's searching for the wording in the article. "Oh, here it is," she says, "Wow, I remember the conversation we were having when I said this!"

"Just read it already, Brynne," I say, spritzing myself with vanilla body spray.

"Okay, fine." She clears her throat with enthusiasm. "It says, 'It's authenticity that attracts people—the right kind of people. In the end, when all the smoke clears, we see who's the real deal.' We were talking about Shanice when I said this—"

"—I know," I interrupt.

"Well, anyhow, I just had to call and thank you. My mom is going to frame the article for me as a keepsake."

"Ah," I say. "I'm touched."

I hadn't won Mrs. Monroe's writing contest after all, but Brynne's excitement over the article means far more to me. There will be other writing opportunities, but only one chance to write about Brynne.

I'd finished dressing and now needed to go dig out a pair of shoes.

"Listen, Miss Celebrity Valedictorian. I gotta go. Dad's taking me to shop for a new computer."

"Okay," Brynne says. "I'll call you later!"

I hear my dad hollering for me just as she ends the call.

～

"THIS IS FOR ME?" I say, cradling the box containing Sony wireless headphones. They're my favorite color too: blue.

"I love them!"

"Yes, dummy, they're for you. Who else would they be for?" Tessa gives me a pointed look.

"I know it's a little early and you aren't leaving just yet, but they were on sale, so I bought them. Hopefully you won't get an obnoxious roommate, but if you do . . ." She throws both hands out toward the headphone box I'm holding.

"Presto! You can block the world out."

I bound over and wrap Tessa in a huge bear hug.

"Thank you so much! If I have an obnoxious roommate, I'll just call you, and you can come evict her for me."

"Ha." She smirks. "Nope. You're on your own."

The excitement dies down, and sadness moves in to take its place. This wasn't how I envisioned going off to college —without Tessa. She must notice the change come over me because she says, "Stop, Alli. We aren't doing this."

I plaster on a fake smile, because what I'm really feeling is that my chest is caving in on itself. But she's right. We aren't doing this.

I'm not doing this. To her.

"Okay, I got this," I say with all the enthusiasm I can muster. I have to coax this train onto another track or risk losing my cool altogether.

"So," I say, setting the headphones aside and sitting on the floor. I wrap my arms around my knees as I face her.

"Are you and Kristin gonna be best friends now? You'll be the only two left here holding down the fort in Tucson."

One of her eyebrows lifts, and she gives me a dirty look.

"Do I *need* another best friend? Are you trying to tell me something?"

I smile and wiggle my eyebrows. "Just checking. Gotta make sure you don't flake out on me."

"Yeah, like I'm gonna throw away almost ten years of training you," she says with a sniff. "I've got too much invested here. You owe me a return on that investment."

Throwing my head back, I laugh.

"Sooooo inaccurate. Who did the training here? Who's the one who taught you how to ride a skateboard?"

"And I should thank you for breaking my arm?" she says.

"Hey, it's not my fault you're a slow learner. What about the time I shoved that boy off the teeter-totter because he was hogging it for too long and you wanted a turn?" I offer.

"Do they even have those on playgrounds anymore?" She asks. "Okay, that's true. I do owe you for that one."

We fall silent and stare at each other.

"I'm gonna miss you, Alli-dork," she says.

"I'm gonna miss you more, Tessa-nerd."

"We said we weren't gonna do this, remember?" she sighs, but she's blinking back tears.

"As I remember, it was *you* who said we weren't gonna

do this—not me," I say. "Besides, you know I always end up doing whatever you do."

There's no use fighting it. We let the tears flow and share memories and laughter for the rest of the night.

Because that's just what best friends do.

Chapter Thirty-Six

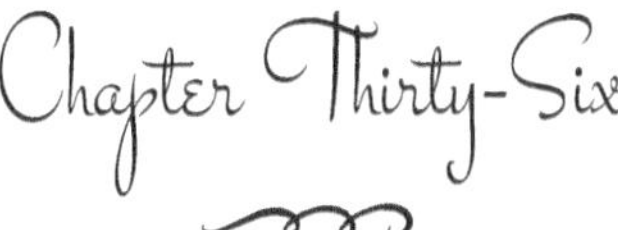

"No."

Anthony stares at me, a look of shock on his handsome face as he takes in the single-word answer.

I hadn't meant it to come out the way it did, but I hadn't expected his question either. It's not fair. I hadn't had time to practice what I wanted to say to him yet. I thought I had more time.

"Oh, Anthony. That sounded horrible. I'm sorry. I didn't mean for it to come out that way. It's just that . . . I like you; I really do. Please don't feel like I've led you on or anything."

I know I'm messing this up big time, and the harder I try to correct it, the more of a mess I'm making.

"It's because, well, I'm leaving."

His eyes widen and he presses one hand against his chest. "*Leaving?*"

I barely move my head when I nod.

"Yeah, I'm leaving Tucson." I groan and try again. "For college. I'm moving to California to attend USC."

"Oh," he says. His head bobs like he gets it, but his face looks more confused than ever.

"That's a good thing, I guess."

His expression reveals that he thinks the idea is anything but *good*.

I move closer, hoping the intimacy reflects what I'm failing miserably to express with words.

"I really like you," I repeat. "I've actually liked you for a long time. Longer than I think I even realized myself. It's just that I don't want things to get more serious for us—not right now anyway—with me going away to college in a few months. I mean, what would be the point, right?"

Anthony pushes his hands down into his pockets and his face softens, the shock wearing off as my explanation washes over him.

"I like you too, Alli. Have for a long time, too, but, unlike you, I've known it the whole time."

His smile is infectious, and I feel myself offering my own sad smile in return.

"I understand how you feel, and it sounds like you have a lot of changes coming at you right now. I hadn't realized that you'd planned to go off to college—"

"—No one really knew," I interrupt. "In fact, my parents didn't even know my final decision until recently."

He nods. "Understood."

Anthony looks deep into my eyes, and, suddenly, the intimate space between us makes me feel panicky. I take the tiniest step backward, hoping he won't notice.

"We don't have to be official or anything, Alli. I get that. You're not ready to start a serious relationship and add a boyfriend to your list of things to attend to."

He smiles at his attempt at humor.

"But I'm willing to wait until, you know, you get settled, and we can talk about it again. When you're ready—*if* you are ever ready."

He keeps his eyes locked on mine, as if trying to read hope and agreement there.

Again, I hadn't expected this.

That Anthony would drop the whole "Can we make our relationship official?" question on me. If I wasn't going to college, would I have fallen all over myself saying "Yes!" to his request? Hadn't I recognized that things between us were heading that way?

I've known Anthony for years and have always understood that he would never invest personal time in a girl unless he was one hundred percent interested. Anthony doesn't play games. I'm honored by his request . . . and scared to death. I've been praying about college, and about Anthony and me, for a while now, and there'd been no banners in the sky or angels at my bedside to tell me what to do.

So I'd decided that college was what was best for me. Starting over. A fresh start. New friends. The whole idea of leaving everything behind that had been a thorn in my side.

So why is this one hiccup throwing me over a cliff?

Anthony and I could still be friends. We could write, and I'll be home for holidays and probably several long weekends. We'd see each other often enough and could figure out if we still felt the same after all that, right?

I can't stay here in Tucson just for Anthony. Or Tessa. Or for anyone else.

What if we didn't work out and I wasted a whole semester or even a school year on a relationship that went up in smoke? I'd waste scholarship money and my parents' financial investment and end up far behind my peers.

Not to mention the blow to my pride when it would become known that Anthony and I didn't work out. Especially since he would be my first real boyfriend after going through my high school career without having had one serious relationship. It seems like most of my peers have claimed to have fallen in love at least once or twice in the four years of high school.

Chad Barton doesn't count.

That short fling was a farce, and the joke was on me. Part of me wonders if I'd at least experienced a few crushes and been on a few dates, would I've been as gullible with Chad?

But the past is the past, and all I want to do is move on. Which is why I want to go away to college—the key word being *away*. I'm not running from my problems, just processing them somewhere else for a while.

Anthony's still watching me, waiting for my answer, trying to gauge if there's a spark of hope or if he should just go ahead and bow out gracefully with his pride still intact.

I tuck my chin and smile sadly up at him. There's a knot in my throat, and I'm so close to grabbing his hand and saying, "Let's do this. College can wait."

I'm torn because I really want to build something with Anthony. He's a great guy and everything I could have hoped for—that any girl could want—in a boyfriend. He's godly, gentle, loyal, consistent, moral, honorable . . . Let's just say there's more *good* things about Anthony Carter than *not* good, and I fear I'm making a big mistake in jeopardizing losing him completely.

But I'm done with fighting the indecision.

I'm going.

"Let's keep it as friends for now and see what happens."

My voice cracks on the last words, and I have to clear my throat before I can go on.

"I'll be back in the fall and, well, I'd love to get together then and hang out."

I know that sounds lame. It's what people say when they both know that they won't make much effort to keep in touch and know it. The words sound hollow and patronizing. That's not how I want to end this at all because I really don't want to sever my connection with him. I know that might happen anyway and that he won't want to wait around for me to figure things out, but it's a chance I have to take.

"But we can talk on the phone, like every day, and I want to hear all about—"

"—Alli," he laughs. "It's okay. Honest. Yes, of course I'll call." His eyebrows lift. "Can I really call *every day*?"

The air feels lighter, and his comforting words become the first stitches pulling my heart back together. I risk touching his arm because I need that physical contact to assure him of my sincerity and because it's the best I can do right now. What I really want to do is throw myself in his arms and cry, but that wouldn't do either one of us any good.

Anthony reaches up and meets my hand on his arm, gripping my fingers in his. The urge to lean in and rest my head on his chest is strong, but I resist. I know it would be the wrong move.

But I'll feel his fingers on mine for months to come, and that will have to be enough.

I lose myself in his gaze. "Yes, every single day."

He gives my fingers a squeeze.

"Well, since you've given me permission, expect me to harass you *every single day*."

He has no idea how much I pray he keeps that promise.

Chapter Thirty-Seven

I'VE NEVER REALLY TAKEN THE TIME TO NOTICE ALL OF THE beautiful trees in our neighborhood before.

The way their branches strain toward each other over the narrow street and form a tunnel of thick foliage that blocks out most of the sunlight. It's like nature is wrapping her arms around me in a warm hug.

I've grown up hearing the neighbors, especially Mr. Ender, complain about the carpet of yellow flowers and dry, brown pods that litter the yards and streets as far as the eye can see.

I never paid much attention when people in the neighborhood were sweeping tree droppings into piles on the sidewalks and driveways to be scooped into trash bins. Some chose to just strap on leaf blowers and swoosh the flowers and leaves into the street gutters and be done with it. But it only took one powerful gust of wind to scatter the whole colorful mess back where it came from.

I've always found the blanket of yellow flowers lovely, but I'm also not the one cleaning up the mess either.

I guess I've never appreciated the warm welcomeness and comforting familiarity of where I live because I've never made the time to take a leisurely stroll around my neighborhood.

What teenage girl has time for nature walks anyway?

But with finals this Thursday and graduation next week, I guess I'm feeling nostalgic. A familiar quote comes to mind: "You never know what you have until it's gone."

Or—in my case—*about* to be gone.

For a while anyway.

I know these trees, this neighborhood, my family and friends—those who aren't heading off to college and new experiences like I am—and everything familiar will all be here when I come home to visit.

Home.

I've been working toward, struggling with, and questioning myself about getting out of Tucson and starting over in a new place for months. Suddenly, I'm already looking for the ruby slippers in case I chicken out in California and decide that "there's no place like home."

"God, I need a little reassurance here."

The words are just a whisper under my breath, but I feel like screaming them from the top of a skyscraper. My thoughts replay the reel of excuses and reasons that I've played in my head over and over so many times that they haunt my dreams at night.

Tessa's doing great and making progress in her healing, and that brings me a lot of peace.

Brynne is leaving a few days after graduation to follow her own dreams.

I know Mom and Dad are nervous about my decision, but they support me.

The only unfinished business on my list is Anthony, but neither of us knows where to go with that yet. We'll just have to figure things out as we go.

I suck in a deep breath of the fragrant Palo Verde blossoms and try to clear my thoughts.

The yellow flowers flutter at my feet as I walk and think about how my mom always complained that the flowers made her sneeze.

When we studied the southwest desert of Arizona in science, I remember Mr. Martin telling us that the Palo Verde became the state tree in 1954 and that you can eat the seeds and flowers, not that any of us have dared to test that claim. Palo Verde trees can also live for over one hundred years.

I don't know why, but I almost giggle thinking about how poor Mr. Ender's great-grandchildren may inherit the task of sweeping up blossoms for years to come. I can imagine them grumbling just as much as he does.

My phone buzzes in my pocket, tugging me back to

reality. Peering down at the screen, I see a text from Brynne:

> Hey! On my way over. I need 2 borrow that tote bag after all. SEE YA!

I smile and tap out a reply:

> Told u you would change ur mind. U owe me Starbucks! :)

I don't wait for her reply. Most likely, she'll just send me an irritated emoji face.

Slipping the phone back into my pocket, I pause and stare at my house.

My home.

Tucson will always be home.

No matter where I go or how far I drift to find my way in life, I'll always have a place to come back to.

See you soon, California.

Did You Enjoy This Book?

~

If you enjoyed this book, I hope you will consider leaving a review on Amazon. Reviews are so important to an author. Even just a line or two can make a huge impact!

WWW.AMAZON.COM/DP/B0BXQMFWXP

SUBSCRIBE TO NEWSLETTER: WWW.RLFELTY.COM/NEWSLETTER

BOOK ONE OF PROVERB'S DAUGHTERS TRILOGY

EBOOKS ARE AVAILABLE THROUGH AMAZON.

PRINTED VERSIONS AVAILABLE AT AMAZON, BARNES & NOBLE, TARGET, AND OTHER BOOKSELLERS.

www.ingramcontent.com/pod-product-compliance
Lightning Source LLC
Chambersburg PA
CBHW030921210726
48290CB00007B/2025